Copyright © 2021 Chencia C. Higgins

www.therealchencia.com

This book is a work of fiction. The names, characters, places and incidents are products of the writers' imagination, or have been used in a fictitious manner. Any resemblance to persons, living or dead, actual events, locations, or organizations is entirely coincidental. No part of this book may be reproduced in any manner without written permission from the author except in the case of brief quotation embodied in critical articles or reviews. All rights reserved.

BEYOND BENEFRIENDS

A FRIEND IN NEED BOOK 2

CHENCIA C. HIGGINS

EKOL MEDIA

ALSO BY CHENCIA C. HIGGINS

JustOneNight.com Novella Series:

No Strings Allowed - Book 1

No Love Allowed - Book 2

The Week Before Forever – Book 2.5

No Games Allowed - Book 3

Holiday Honey – Book 4

K.S.L. – Book 5

The Vow Series:

To Buy a Vow – Book 1

To Build a Vow – Book 2

To Break a Vow – Book 3

Things Hoped For – Book 4

Wolves of West Texas Series:

Janine: His True Alpha – Book 1

Lenora: His Omega Mate – Book 2

Alicia: His Troublesome Fate – Book 3

The Color Spectrum Duet:

The Color Spectrum: Ebony

<u>A Friend In Need</u>

Benefriends

Beyond Benefriends

<u>Black Family Saga:</u>

Glasses

Fast Breaker

<u>The Luminous Cruse Chronicles:</u>

Love On The Luminous

<u>Boos & Booze</u>

Costume Cutty

<u>Standalones:</u>

Her & Them

Remember Our Love

Loud & Lew'd

An Illicit Seduction

Consolation Gifts

I'm glad these two finally got it together.
I hope that you enjoy their journey.

ONE

TESTING THE WATERS

I'd gotten off a lot of jokes at their expense, but the truth was that Shad and Aisha deciding to hook up didn't affect the crew at all. Not in a good way; not in a bad way. It just...was. They'd been together for almost two years, and things were as normal as ever. The six of us still hung out once a month for our kickback, and Shad continued to invite us to tag along while he covered different concerts for the Browntown Weekly. The only marked difference was that Darwin's wife, Carrie, occasionally joined us for the kickback, but she got on with everyone like a house on fire, so even that didn't feel like a change.

Shad and Aisha weren't overly affectionate in front of us—which was definitely due to Aisha being naturally low-key, not at all the result of a complaint

—and no one made a big deal about them getting together. Not even Monie, who had been the most vocal when we all found out. The only thing that seemed to be different, even internally…was me.

Shad finally going after what Darwin and I been knew he'd always wanted was fucking with my head. The girls were our friends—our *best* friends. They were family. We weren't supposed to fuck up the family dynamic by introducing our dicks to the party. But…if Shad did it and came out a winner, then maybe the feelings I'd buried and thoughts I'd ignored could…

"Yo, fool! Are you playing your hand or what?!"

Yanked out of my thoughts, I snapped my head to the right and glared at my brother, who was staring me down with a scowl on his face.

Smirking, I swiped my thumb across the cards in my hand, eying the sole card that sat in the middle of the rickety card table that I'd had since we were in college. The dorms had been sparsely furnished, without any viable options for the many cards and domino games that I tended to host. At this point, the table was more nostalgic than functional, but I planned to hold on to it until it collapsed into a pile of plywood and foam.

"Aye, nigga! Don't worry about how I'm moving with my hand." Removing an eight of spades from my hand, I slapped it onto the six of spades that Darwin had tossed out. "Now, play that!"

To my left, Lisette rolled her eyes and tossed a nine of spades on top of my card. "You really thought you were doing something, slapping that card down like that. Calm down, fool."

I shook my head. *Fucking amateurs.* "Oh, I was definitely doing something. Wait on it." Instead of looking at my partner, I stared at the table, doing what I'd instructed Lisette to do.

The wait was a short one. Monie flicked a Jack of Spades onto the pile and then immediately scooped up the four cards and neatly added them to the five books near her elbow. I jumped up and beat on my chest.

"That's what the fuck I'm talkin' about! Show them how we do, Mo!"

"Sitcho' cuckoo for Cocoa Puffs ass down," Darwin grumbled. "It was one damn book."

"Exactly," chimed Lis. "You're acting like y'all won the game."

I chuckled and slid back into my seat. "You bid seven, remember? So unless you or Darkwing Duck are holding both jokers in your hands, you done already lost."

Monie smirked but didn't say a word. It was a small movement that—thankfully—only I seemed to catch, and it made me think that she probably held at least one of those aforementioned jokers in her hand. This game was ours.

"Or a two!" yelled Shad from his comfortable position on the couch next to Aisha. They were chillin', sitting with less than a foot of space between them, with her hand was on his thigh, and his arm was behind her head while they waited to play whoever won this round.

Gasping, I turned to face him. "The hell you just say, bro?"

"Deuces are wild!" he repeated, a goofy grin on his face that told me he was aggin' on purpose.

"Deuces are—*hell naw*! Not in my African American household!"

Everyone but Darwin busted out laughing. He mugged me, lip curling in annoyance. He was good and mad, which meant he knew there was no chance for him to win. A smile as wide as his forehead stretched across my face.

"Play your damn hand!" he snapped, making me cheese even harder.

Turning my attention back to the table, I examined the two cards already tossed out. There was a three of spades and a two of hearts on the table, with the red card partially covering the black card. I looked from Monie to my brother, noting the passive expressions they each wore, neither giving anything away. Silently, I removed a card from the last three in my hand and tossed it onto the pile.

If they were feeling froggy, I was gonna make them jump.

I regarded Lisette and damn near shot out of my seat to crow my victory. She looked sick. Eyes wide and uncertain as she stared at the pile of cards. There was absolutely no way she had anything of value in her hands.

"C'mon, Lis," Monie urged. "Staring at them won't make a miracle happen. Just throw something out so we can move on."

Darwin sucked his teeth. "Leave the shit-talking to Vick." Then he offered Lisette a wan smile. "Go ahead, Lis."

With an audible click, she swallowed hard, removed a card from her hand, and delicately placed it atop the pile. Her hand hovered for a few seconds as if she was afraid to let us see what she'd played. When she retracted her hand, we all leaned forward in anticipation.

Ace of Spades.

Ordinarily, it would be a great card to play, but with my low Joker already ruling the table, it was as useless as the two of hearts her partner had already played.

"Fuck," Darwin whispered, throwing his remaining cards down, and sitting back in his chair as he dragged both of his hands down his face.

There was no need to keep playing; the game was over. They'd needed seven books to force another round, but instead, they overbid and lost. Monie and I were advancing to the next round, which we would undoubtedly win because Aisha was just as terrible at playing Spades as Lisette was. As a matter of fact, Lisette and Aisha were usually partners when we all played. Darwin and Shad had been partners since we were in college, but once Shad and Aisha got together, Aisha asked to be Shad's partner. He'd consented, but now, every time we got ready to play, Darwin and Shad acted like they were Celie and Nettie being ripped apart. The rest is history.

When everyone's remaining cards were flipped over, it was quite obvious that the last two books would go to me and Monie. I pushed back from the table, jumped to my feet, and ran around my living room.

"Let's goooooo!" I yelled at the top of my lungs. "Let's fucking go!"

Pulling my shirt over my head, I tossed it onto the couch beside Aisha and stood in front of her and Shad while doing an exaggerated crab flex as if I was a bodybuilder. Darwin got up and stormed into the kitchen, prompting me to approach the table. First, I hugged Lisette, wrapping my arms around her from behind and rubbing my cheek against hers.

"Thanks, baby doll," I chirped gleefully, dropping a wet kiss onto her cheek. Groaning, she slapped at me erratically, shooing me away from her.

"Man, get out of here!" She got up from the table and followed Darwin into the kitchen.

Laughing, I moved over to Monie, enveloping her in a similar embrace.

"You killed that shit, girl. That's why you're my partner for life!"

Shaking her head, Monie leaned forward and began to gather up the cards from the center of the table.

"I'm your partner for life because I'm the only one that can stand to be paired up with your silly ass."

"You're saying it like that's a bad thing," I countered, nuzzling her neck. "Sounds like fate to me."

"Whatever," she laughed, shaking her head.

When she started shuffling the cards, I dropped a quick kiss onto the sliver of skin just below her ear. Instantly, she froze. I waited for her reaction, wondering if I was going to catch an elbow to the gut or if she'd keep on as if nothing had happened. It was neither of those. Monie canted her head to the side and eyed me suspiciously.

"What are you doing, Vick?" she queried in a low, cautious voice.

Grinning, I kissed her again. "Just tryna see something," I murmured.

"And what exactly are you trying to see?"

Glancing up, I met her eyes. They were unreadable and her face was carefully blank. "If you feel as good in my arms as you did in my dreams last night."

Her eyes widened slightly, and then she busted out laughing. Shrugging me off of her, she shook her head again and stood from the table.

"Shad get your boy. He's feeling frisky and being corny."

Laughing, I reclaimed my seat and linked my hands behind my head.

"Shad, tell Mo to stop smelling so good. Her pheromones are calling out to me."

Lisette reentered the living room and plopped down onto the couch. "I told you that new perfume was going to attract strays," she giggled.

Pursing her lips, Monie shot me a weird look before disappearing into the bathroom.

"Is he misbehaving again?"

Darwin finally emerged from my kitchen and nodded toward me. In his hands was the opaque spray bottle that I used for watering my plants.

"What the fuck?!" I stammered, laughing as I held up a hand for a shield when he aimed the nozzle in my direction. "Go put that shit back under my damn sink!"

Instead of following my damn instructions, he moved closer. "If you're out here acting like a dog, I'm gonna treat you like one." Depressing the nozzle, he attempted to hit me in the face, but a fine mist came out instead of the sharp stream that he likely expected.

Laughing so hard that tears came to my eyes, I reached up and snatched the bottle out of his hands. He didn't even resist, just rubbed his head as he howled with laughter and took a seat. I motioned to Shad and Aisha.

"Bring y'all asses over here and get this spanking."

"Oh, Lord," Aisha mumbled, stepping over Lisette's legs to make her way toward the chair that Lisette had vacated. "Be gentle, please."

Shaking my head, I began dealing the cards. "Sorry, Eesh. I'm only gentle in the bedroom." The door to the bathroom opened, and Monie headed toward the card table. "Ain't that right, Mo?"

Without glancing in my direction, she sat down across from me and snatched up her cards in one smooth movement. "I wouldn't know," she offered, nonchalantly, "you're not big enough to ride this ride."

"Shit!" Darwin yelped, eyes wide as he sat forward and turned my way. "I felt the heat from that burn."

Chuckling, I began grouping my cards by suit. "I can guarantee that you would find parts of me to be the perfect size."

Amusement twinkled in Darwin's eyes as he flicked his gaze from me to Monie. "*Finish him,*" he instructed ominously, in Shao Kahn style.

A smile flirted at the corner of Monie's lips, but she never took her eyes off of her cards as she shuffled them around into an order that worked for her. "I was waiting on you to bulk up, baby boy, but it turns out that you don't like eating your Wheaties."

"*Fatality,*" Darwin intoned victoriously.

Brows furrowed, I turned my cards face-down. "That's just because I prefer eating something else. Keep playing, Mo, and I'll have you climbing the walls."

Lisette sat forward on the couch, volleying her head between Monie and me. "Wait. Are we still joking around or..."

"Right," Aisha added, giving Monie a pointed look that Monie promptly ignored. Turning to me,

Aisha asked, "What's tea, Vick? You tryna upgrade from a Happy Meal to a prime rib or nah?"

"Well—"

"*Anyways,*" Monie interjected, smoothly changing the subject as the game began, "I've been nominated for best makeup artist on a continuing series and I need a date to the awards show next month. Who's available?"

"Oh! Pick me!" Lisette bounced on the couch with her hand in the air. "You know I *love* an opportunity to get dolled-up."

Nodding, Monie tossed a card into the center of the table. "Send me a picture of your dress so I can prep your beat."

"Will do."

I slapped a card onto the table, causing Aisha to cringe as I swiped all four cards toward Monie.

"Oof!" she said apologetically, giving Shad a shameful look. "Sorry, babe."

Shad pursed his lips and nodded. "It's all good, Eesh."

Slapping my hand on the table, I yelled, "No talking across the board!"

Darwin groaned. "Calm your ass down, Vick!"

"I told y'all we should have picked a less competitive game this month," Shad murmured out of the corner of his mouth.

"If the game has a winner, he's going to be competitive," commented Monie. "Just up your skills, and it won't be a problem. No offense, Eesh."

Aisha shrugged. "None taken, boo."

"Yeah, punk," I added, raising my eyebrows at Shad. "Up your skills!" I kept my face impassive as I heckled him, but inside I was grinning like a Cheshire cat as I listened to Monie defend me.

"What date is the event?" Lisette chirped, probably in an attempt to steer the conversation in another direction.

"January tenth."

"Ooh, okay." She pulled out her phone. "That's a Sunday, right?"

Eyes on the board, Monie nodded. "Mmhm."

"Wait," Shad interjected, looking over his shoulder at Lisette. "That won't work. You're supposed to be going to that Tank and the Bangas show with me that day."

Lisette's eyes widened and she snapped her fingers. "I completely forgot! My bad."

"It's fine," Shad assured her, "I can take someone else."

Since the game was obviously on pause, I finally spoke up. "You can take me," I informed Shad. "They're a dope band, plus I'd love to get a closer look at Tank's fine ass. Did they give you backstage passes this time?" Shad wasn't always provided the opportunity to speak with the artist after a show, but when he did, it was an amazing time.

"Man, I really wanted to see them, though!" Lisette pouted.

"Well, why don't you go to the event with Monie, Vick?" Darwin suggested. "Then Lis can keep her commitment to Shad."

"This is a *professional* event," Monie countered. "Taking Vick is like bringing a puppy to church; a disaster waiting to happen."

Everyone laughed and I smirked. Monie had yet to look my way since she'd sat back down, but from the way she had twisted in her seat and crossed her legs, I could tell that she was saying one thing but thinking something completely different. My words —my attention—were doing something to her.

"So, what you're saying is that you want me to hump your leg?"

"Dawg!" Shad doubled over, clutching at his sides as he howled with laughter. "You gotta chill, bruh."

"I'm chillin', fam. I promise."

Aisha giggled. "You are such a pig, Vick."

I snorted. "Oink, oink."

"Where's that damn spray bottle?" Darwin inquired darkly.

"Don't worry about it," Monie assured, her tone

saccharine sweet and infused with levity, "I've got a roll of newspaper with his name on it."

Gasping, I brought a hand to my chest and turned to my brother. "You told Harpo to beat me!"

"Bruh," laughed Shad, "please play the game!"

Lifting my hands into the air, I nodded. "Okay, okay. Damn." The game resumed, and Monie and I were three books into our inevitable win when I glanced up at her.

"All jokes aside, Mo. I'll roll with you to the event."

Finally, she gave me those gorgeous brown eyes, lifting her focus from the cards in the center of the table to give me her undivided attention. She didn't say anything for a beat, just stared at me. I lifted a brow in question, wondering what was going through her mind at that moment. But then she nodded and bent her head again.

Her lack of words didn't faze me. I knew Mo, and because I knew her, I understood that she was likely trying to work out how to handle me. My interest in her hadn't been subtle, yet it wasn't as overt as the crew seemed to expect me to be with women, which probably had her confused. I'd been giving her time to adjust to my attention, but the transition was apparently too slow. Now it was time to move into phase two.

TWO

RESOLUTIONS

My boy was finally about to pop the question and I was hype like I was the one about to get engaged. He'd chosen the best day of the year to do it, in my opinion. New Year's Day, right after the clock struck midnight was the perfect moment to ask the love of your life to become your official road dog —complete with matching last names. We usually did the celebration thing at my brother's house, so Shad had filled Darwin and me in on the plan, which kicked off a few minutes before the countdown was to start. Glancing at my watch, I headed into the kitchen where my brother had lined up trays piled high with the food Carrie, who was a chef, cooked. Instead of grabbing the pre-sliced French bread and stuffing it with fried shrimp and remoulade sauce, I plucked two praline-topped brownies from the tray marked "edibles" and did a little jig as I bit into one.

"Nobody told me the party was in here."

Still dancing, I spun around and grinned at the woman who stood in the doorway with her hands propped on her hips. I was unsurprised that Vivian had once again found her way toward me. She was one of Carrie's line sisters who had moved out of town after graduation and never moved back. We'd hooked up a few times in the past when she came to visit, but it had been more than a year since we'd last seen each other. Although she'd been the one to put a stop to our hookups, she'd been giving me a look all night that said she wouldn't mind if I brought in the new year by ringing her bell. If I didn't already have plans to have someone else in my arms when the clock struck midnight, I might've been interested. As it were, the past was the past.

Winking, I turned to put the second brownie on a plate. "As long as you've known Carrie, you should know by now that the party is wherever her cooking is."

Tilting her head to the side, Vivian eyed me up and down. "I'm talking about the party in here; the one where you're the star."

There was no mistaking the hungry look in her eyes, and she was climbing out of the casual hints pool and dipping her toe into the outright suggestive hot tub. Chuckling, I shook my head.

"I'm nobody's star, Viv. At best, I'm a supporting cast member. At worst, I'm an understudy."

Dropping her hands to her side, Vivian sauntered into the kitchen, heading straight for me. Placing the plated brownie on the counter, I popped the remainder of the one I'd been eating into my mouth and crossed my arms over my chest. Vivian stopped directly in front of me, so close that if she would have hiccupped, her titties would have brushed my forearms. When our eyes met, she pouted.

"You've been avoiding me all night, Vick. I'm starting to take it personally." With her lips poked out and her eyes wide, she gave off this air of sexy and innocent that made me smirk since I knew for a fact only one of those things embodied her.

The last time we'd spoken, Vivian informed me that she was no longer interested in maintaining a "long-distance situationship", bringing an end to our nameless—but convenient and mutually satisfying— arrangement. She'd made sure to let me know from the jump that we were just having fun, so I knew it was only temporary and hadn't sweat her about it. I hadn't heard from her since then, and for her to be in my face now, pulling a whole-ass one-eighty was funny to me. Vivian dropped her hands to my waist and leaned closer, officially putting her titties on my chest, resting them on my arms as if I was her support bra.

"So," she murmured seductively, "what's up?"

Lifting my shoulders, I made a noncommittal noise in my throat. "Nothing's up."

She blinked from underneath thick eyelashes and somehow turned her lips down even further.

"What do you mean 'nothing'?"

I shrugged again. "You put a halt to what we had going on way back when, so I'm not playing games or doing any simple shit like that when I say 'nothing's up'. I'm just respecting the boundaries that you set out. *You* said we were through, so we're through."

Licking her lips, she dropped her hands from my waist and frowned.

"But…"

"Oh, my bad y'all."

We both looked toward the entrance to see Monie standing there with an empty plate in her hand. Her eyes roved over the both of us before she lifted an eyebrow, giving me an indecipherable look before backing out of the kitchen and disappearing down the hall in which she'd come.

"Aye, Mo! Wait up!"

Twisting, I grabbed the plated brownie off of the counter and slipped around Vivian to go after Monie.

When I hit the hallway, I was pleasantly surprised to find that she'd stopped just before reaching the door to the garage. Smirking, she met my eyes and shook her head in admonishment.

"Why'd you leave her in there like that?"

Ignoring her question, I wrapped an arm around her shoulder and handed her the brownie I held in my free hand.

"Here."

I waited for her to take the offering before I removed the empty plate from her other hand and held it at my side.

Immediately, her lips spread in a delighted grin, looking from the decadent treat to me. "How'd you know I was coming in there for this?"

"Shit, you said you wanted to go to new heights in 2021, so I figured this was a good way to start."

Laughing, she pushed my arm off of her shoulder and pulled open the door, stepping out into the garage to get to the huge tent in Darwin and Carrie's front yard. They'd set up tables, chairs, and ice-filled tubs of beverages for the crowd of people that they'd invited over. A DJ was stationed at the front door for ease of running extension cords, so all traffic was routed through the opened garage.

"Since you know so damn much," she sassed,

"you should have gone ahead and cut it up so I could share it with Aisha and Lisette."

Pursing my lips, I gave her wild a look. "Cut it up for what? You can eat the whole thing like I did."

Gasping, Monie spun around and stared at me, her mouth hanging open in shock.

"Vick, no! You're not supposed to eat the whole thing!"

Sucking my teeth, I kept walking. "That's only for the inexperienced. Ya boy has a tolerance as high as Everest."

"If by Everest, you mean Everest Institute, and by high you mean tuition, then I might believe you." She pushed at my shoulder from behind, and I could tell from the attitude in her voice that she was probably rolling her eyes at my back.

"Don't come calling me when you can't even focus enough to walk in a straight line. And when little blue bunnies are hopping around asking you for change to get on the bus, don't say I didn't warn you."

Grabbing her hand, I tugged her in front of me and tucked her back under my arm. Monie was tall as hell, standing just a couple of inches shorter than me when she was barefoot, and I was six-three. The ability to look right into her face when we spoke was one of the many things I appreciated about her. With only a slight tilt of my chin, my mouth was near her ear, allowing me to keep my tone low as I uttered words meant only for her ears.

"If I say I got it, then I got it. Why don't you let me be the judge of what I can handle, aight?"

The slow bob of her throat as she swallowed caught my eye, and I watched her warm-brown gaze find my face before falling to my lips and hovering there for several seconds. Realizing that the heat I saw in those depths was for me, and me alone, brought a slow grin to my face. The curving of my lips must've shaken her out of her thoughts because her eyes immediately snapped up to meet mine. I was unable to wipe away the silly grin, and she expelled an annoyed groan, followed by lobbing a heavy slap to my shoulder. She shoved away from me and stomped over to the tent where the crew was scattered, allowing the perfect opportunity to admire her curvaceousness.

It was a balmy sixty degrees outside, and since this was a casual thing with only the crew, our immediate families, and a handful of friends present, Monie wore a yellow t-shirt dress that stopped mid-thigh, paired with a cropped denim jacket and knee-high boots. Her thick hair was braided down in the front and pulled into a massive puffball in the back, and her face was bare, save for lipstick and eye shadow. She was dressed down and comfortable and had just looked at me like she wanted to kiss me.

It had only been two weeks since the kickback and phase two was in full effect.

Over the next hour, I kicked it with my people as the effects of the brownie washed over me. As I'd told Monie, I knew what I could handle, and instead of paranoia, I felt mellow as fuck. I was chilled all the way out, giddy as shit, and feeling positive about the new year. It was going to be my year, starting with leaning into the belief that whatever you're doing when the year begins is what you'll be doing all year.

"It's almost time!"

Blinking, I watched as Darwin rushed past me after muttering the announcement in my direction. We were five minutes from the start of the count-down, and each of us had a job to do. Darwin grabbed Carrie around the waist just as Carrie began tugging on Vivian's arm. The three of them stepped from under the tent and hovered near the farthest opening away from the garage. Next, Lisette latched hands with the woman she'd brought with her, and led her over near Darwin, stopping about six feet away from his group.

Following their lead, I moved to where Monie sat in conversation with Aisha and my parents. Leaning over the back of her chair, I propped my chin on her shoulder and pressed my face into the soft skin of her neck visible above the neckline of the jacket. She jumped at the contact, bending to the side and lifting her shoulder in an attempt to knock me off. It was fruitless since I just moved with her.

"Boy!" she shrieked, her eyes darting over to the other occupants under the tent. "What are you doing?!"

"Come with me," I murmured against her neck, reaching around her to grip the table on either side of her body, effectively caging her in.

Even zooted, I didn't miss the way she shuddered when I spoke, and I didn't say a word when she sucked in a breath, shaking her shoulders to play off her involuntary reaction.

"Do you have to be all up on me to ask that?" she questioned, voice dripping with sophisticated annoyance.

Aisha busted out laughing, while my mama just shook her head, a knowing look in her eye as she stared at the side of my face before standing and following my dad over to where Darwin stood.

"Get off of her!" Aisha demanded, leaning forward in her seat to slap at one of my hands. "Not everybody wants your bony body poking at them!"

Furrowing my brows, I turned to her. "Yo, why are you coming at me like your man isn't only seven and a half pounds heavier than me? And that's when he's soaking wet!"

Their laughter rang loudly and I grinned, shaking my head as I pressed my face back into Monie's neck and took a deep inhalation. We'd been outside for a few hours but she still managed to smell so damn good.

As if he'd been summoned, Shad appeared under the tent, shaking like a leaf as he bent to whisper something into Aisha's ear before tugging her over toward our friends. Glancing over at my brother, our eyes collided just as he nodded back toward the house. I needed to move, and fast. Releasing my hold on the table, I reached for Monie's hand, tugging her up out of her seat and around the tent to post up by the huge red oak near the street. We were slightly out of the circle that everyone had made, but Monie caught onto the pattern after a moment of observation.

She turned to me with suspicion swimming in her narrowed eyes. "What's going on?"

"We're about to do the countdown," I responded, pulling my bottom lip between my teeth as I stared at her pretty ass cocoa-brown skin and sexy ass lips. Taking notice of my gape, Monie giggled.

"Your ass is high as hell."

Cheesing, I shrugged. "Shiiiid, it's true. But why you say that?"

"'Cause you're staring me down like I'm a T-bone steak, and we all know how your ass loves red meat."

"You look better than a damn steak. Good enough to eat." Just the thought made my mouth water, and I licked my lips to make sure I wasn't drooling. "You probably taste better too."

Nostrils flaring, she shifted her weight from one leg to the other and looked off to the side for a moment. Seconds later, her eyes found mine once more before rolling as if my bawdy compliment had annoyed her. Huffing, she tried to step away from me, but must've forgotten that we were still holding hands. I had no intention of letting her go, so I tugged her back against my chest, spinning her to face the rest of the circle. Then I propped my chin on her shoulder and wrapped my arms around her waist.

Taking a deep breath through her nose, she shook her head as she exhaled. "I swear I'm staying away from your ass the next time you want to eat a whole damn edible. That praline brownie got you out here feel lusty."

Eyelids low, I watched my dad walk around the circle and pass around sparklers. Monie took one, but

I declined, not wanting to remove my arms from around her long enough to hold it.

"I see you, son," he smirked before moving on. Chuckling, I watched as he finished up and returned to my mother's side.

"Stop frontin'," I murmured into Monie's ear. "That brownie might've mellowed me out, but wanting you has nothing to do with that. Let's leave the pretending in 2020, 'cause in 2021 I'm tryna lock that thang down, aight?"

Startled, she twisted her neck to look at me.

"What if I don't want to be locked down?"

I shrugged. "Then you gotta tell me that shit. I can't read your mind, Mo, and you'd prolly find a way to block me even if I could."

"What if—"

Whatever she was going to ask next was interrupted when everyone started yelling out the countdown. I wanted her to finish, but she whipped her head toward the others and lifted her sparkler in the air, so I let the moment go.

"TEN…NINE…EIGHT…SEVEN…SIX…"

Shad gently corralled Aisha into the center of the circle without her noticing, as everyone around them held their lit sparklers high, excitedly counting down the seconds until the new year.

"FIVE...FOUR...THREE...TWO...ONE!   HAPPY NEW YEAR!"

Cheers went up around us, but the only thing on my mind was the woman in my arms. Monie turned back to me almost expectantly, and I stared back unblinkingly, giving her all of the time in the world to step out of my embrace or demand that I back up. She didn't do either.

"Happy New Year, Mo."

"Happy New Year, Vick." Her tone was soft. There was a thin note of nerves, or anticipation, or maybe the very same emotions I felt coursing through my body that underlined her hushed voice.

I felt like she was calling to me without saying a word, and I'd die if I didn't answer her call. So I made a move to save my life. There wasn't much space to cover, and all it took was a short extension of my neck before our lips pressed together. I didn't expect her to kiss me back, but she shocked the hell out of me by twisting a little and shifting her body closer to mine, deepening the kiss with the changed angle. A groan slipped from my lips, and I lowered my hand from her side, digging my fingers into her hip.

That small movement was like a bottle of smelling salts. Monie quickly broke our kiss, stumbling backward out of my grasp. She brought her hand to her mouth, fingers brushing her lips, wide eyes regarding me as if she was unsure of who I was.

Or maybe she was finally seeing me in a new light.

As we stood there staring at each other, I licked my lips, chasing that too-tiny bit of her taste that was left behind on my lips. She sucked in a breath and took a step toward me, but the sound of whooping stole both of our attention. We turned to see Shad drop down to one knee in front of Aisha, whose eyes were wide and glossy as she clapped her hands over her mouth.

Monie squealed and rushed over to them, but I held back to watch the scene unfold. These were new beginnings for many of us, and I hoped Monie was ready because now I was coming for her, full steam ahead.

THREE

CLOSED MOUTHS DON'T GET FED

The night of Monie's event, I insisted that I drive us instead of meeting her at the venue as she'd suggested. When I pulled up to her complex, I shot her a text to let her know I'd arrived, then pocketed my keys as I walked the few yards to her townhouse. She'd responded quickly, letting me know that her door would be unlocked for me, so I let myself inside. After calling out a greeting so that she wouldn't be startled when she came out of her room, I had a seat on her all-white sofa. I hadn't been seated for more than a couple of minutes when I noticed her in my peripheral coming my way.

"I'm almost ready," she assured me as she grabbed a large, black shoulder-bag from the other end of the couch.

My heart thumped double-time as I stared at her

from across the room. If I didn't know better, I would think that Monie was on a mission of her own. I just wasn't sure if I was her prey or an innocent bystander. Monie was beautiful on her worst day, but on a day like today, when she put in the extra effort to glam up? She was breathtaking.

Standing to my feet, I dragged my tongue over my lips as I ate her up with my eyes. Wearing a long-sleeved, ice-blue gown which fell to her ankles in sweeping ruffles, and gave peeks of her long legs and thick, right thigh with every step that she took, she made my mouth water. Pressing a hand to my chest over my rapidly beating heart, I grinned.

"Fuck, Mo. You look sexy as hell."

She beamed at me, plump, glossy lips spreading to reveal white teeth. "Thanks, Vick."

Then she winked before turning on the impossibly thin heels of her matching pumps and sauntering over to the dining area to transfer items from the black bag into the small, ball-shaped clutch bag she'd placed on the table.

"*Mm! Goddamn.*"

Unbidden, the low curse fell from my lips when I caught sight of her exposed back. The dress covered her shoulders and then dipped down to the small of her back, mere inches above her ass, revealing the elaborate elephant head tattoo that covered the top half of her back.

Hearing the sound, which wasn't low enough, Monie shot me a glance over her shoulder, her lips curved into a flirtatious tilt.

"What are you over there making all that noise for?" she asked as if she didn't already know.

"Don't mind me," I murmured with a shallow shrug of my shoulders. "I'm just incapable of staying silent when I see a fantastic piece of art."

Quickly, she turned back toward her bags, but not before I saw her cheeks lift as her smile deepened.

"Boy, hush!"

Since I knew this was a big night for her, I did as she said; choosing to hold my tongue until after she'd won her award. After that, I was too proud of her and her accomplishments to keep quiet about it. Monie had downplayed the event when she mentioned it at the kickback, but the awards were a big deal. There weren't only makeup artists from Houston-based shows in attendance, but also immensely talented people from across the nation who worked on syndicated shows—and even some artists who had worked on movies—and they were all up for the same awards as Monie.

When her name was announced as the winner in her category, several people got on their feet, joining me as I clapped and cheered as she made her way to the stage. Her speech was short and sweet, and when she took her seat next to me, I pulled her into my arms, dropping a soft kiss onto her round cheek.

"I'm proud of you, Mo," I whispered into her ear.

Wordlessly, she stared at me, an undecipherable emotion in her eyes that only disappeared when I raised my eyebrows in question. Then, she shook her head and offered me a smile in return.

"Now you know that my job is serious and that I don't just be playing in makeup all day."

They were already announcing the nominations for the next category, so I chuckled softly before shaking my head and leaning closer to her.

"I've watched enough of those videos that you post on social media to know that you damn sure be playing and having fun, but your results are nothing to joke about. You love what you do, and your skills are evident."

Like a shining star, Monie beamed at me—literally glowed—smiling widely, displaying all of her teeth, eyes crinkled up and damn-near disappearing beneath her thick lashes. But then, as if a switch was flipped, her expression turned suspicious, and she shook my arm off of her shoulders. Cutting her eyes at me, she leaned to her right, trying to put a few inches of space in between us. The reaction was such a stark difference from moments earlier that my eyes furrowed as I gave her a baffled look.

"What was that about?"

Pursing her lips, she crossed her legs and leaned her knees away from me, unintentionally pushing her ass back in my direction. Glancing down at that round mound, I licked my lips before meeting her furious brown eyes.

"Your ass ain't slick," she snapped. "Tryna finesse me outta some pussy with encouragements and affirmations and shit." Curling her lip, she sucked her teeth. "You must think I'm one of those li'l apple-headed girls that be running behind you. Tuh!"

Instantly, a silly grin pulled at my lips.

Reaching across the space she called herself creating, I tugged her back toward me, cheesing even harder at how she melted like a popsicle in the summer once I had my hands on her. Despite how random it was, knowing that she was thinking about us in bed together felt like I'd added another hash mark under my name, and was that much closer to winning her heart. Sliding an arm around her waist, I held her in a firm embrace as I leaned in and nuzzled her neck—a move I was finding steadily addicting. Lifting her shoulder to block me from her neck, she tried faking like she didn't want me on her, but she never pulled out of my arms.

"Chill out, Mo," I chided amicably. "I told you on New Year's that I was gonna be everything you need this year and beyond. If you wanna fuck a nigga, then just say that. I ain't holding out on you, 'cause I swear it's yours for the taking."

She sucked in a breath and turned to me, her eyes low with lust but with obviously-manufactured offense darkening her beautiful face. "That's *not* what I said!"

Nodding, I laughed, unsure if she was trying to convince me or herself. "Yeah, it is. I'm over here complimenting your skills, and you start talking about sex. If that ain't a cry for the dick, then tell me what else that was supposed to be."

Eyes narrowed, she glared at me but didn't say another word for the rest of the ceremony. I let her fume in silence for about fifteen minutes before tugging her toward me again.

"*Now* who's tryna finesse? You're acting up like you want me to punish that ass tonight. Is that what you want?"

When she whipped around to face me, her brown eyes were full of pleading, and want, and—*fuck*! My chest hurt just seeing that shit, and my dick was suddenly hard, and I wanted to give her whatever it was that she could fix her mouth to ask for. But she *had* to ask for it because I'd be damned if I found myself in a similar situation to the one Shad stumbled into when he and Aisha first veered onto that friends-with-benefits path. Things were good for them now, but bro was down bad when he realized he was in love and didn't think his feelings were reciprocated.

I didn't want to waste time with crossed wires and miscommunication when it came to Monie. It was why I'd been upfront with her about where I stood from jump. The ball had always been in her court while I waited on her to make a move. Fittingly, I stared at her, waiting.

She licked her lips and severed our eye contact, subsequently punching my heart in the balls at the same time.

"I—I don't know what I want, Vick."

"Nah," I uttered, shaking my head, "I don't buy that. You know exactly what you want, and if it wasn't me, you wouldn't have a problem saying so. I've seen you shut men down lightning-quick, *and* I remember how you chewed Shad's ass up when you thought he'd wronged Eesh. A cat ain't ever had a grip on your tongue."

Her lips parted, and it was almost like I could see the words sitting on her tongue, wanting to leap out at me.

"So, what's up, Mo?"

"I—"

"Monelle!"

I swallowed down a curse as a woman waved a hand in the air, skirting tables as she headed toward us, effectively ruining the moment and sealing Monie's lips. Looking around, I noticed that several people had stood up and were abandoning the tables in favor of the dance floor and open bar. I'd been so wrapped up in Monie that I hadn't noticed the awards portion come to an end. According to the program we'd been handed when we first arrived, the event was technically over, but the bar was open until two in the morning, and the band didn't leave until then either.

The woman neared, and Monie stood to her feet, causing me to rise reflexively.

"Oh, Monelle!" she exclaimed a little breathlessly as if she'd been rushing to get to our table, "I'm so glad I caught you before you left. Congratulations on your win. You more than deserve it."

Reaching out, she grabbed Monie's hand and took a few deep inhalations through her nose to steady her breathing. From the slight wrinkles around her lips and eyes, it was clear she was an older woman, even though the heavy streak of gray in the front of her shoulder-length hair looked as if it was purposeful and not the result of aging.

Monie smiled at the woman. "Thank you so much, Director. You reached me just in time. We were about to head out." Gesturing to me, she made introductions. "Director Timms, this is my date, Vick. Vick, this is Director Timms. She's over the makeup and costume department at the network and is also known as my boss's boss."

Director Timms eyed me from head to toe, an appreciative gleam in her sharp gaze. "Well, hello, handsome." Arching an eyebrow at Monie, she squeezed Mo's hand again and leaned toward her as if sharing a secret. "I'd be in a hurry to get home too if he was my date."

"Oh, Lord! Please don't pump his head up!"

The director leveled Monie with a knowing smirk. "I'll leave that to you, my dear."

Monie's eyes widened as she glanced back at me, probably trying to see if I'd heard. I bit back a laugh at the look on her face. Maybe that would help her make a decision about us.

"*Anywho*," the director singsonged, "I was hoping to have a quick word with you. Do you have a few minutes?"

Monie nodded. "Yes. Absolutely." She started to walk off but then turned back to me. "Oh, are you going to stay here?" She gestured at the table.

I shook my head and nodded toward the bar in

the back of the room. "I'm gonna grab another drink. Just meet me there when you're done."

Nodding, she took off behind the woman who was, once again, moving like she was about to get a parking ticket and thought she could stop the officer with her good looks. Once they disappeared into a crowd of people, I made my way across the room to the bar. There were several people behind the counter to service everyone, so my wait wasn't long. I'd moved off to the side and was sipping on my bourbon and coke when a veritable brickhouse of a woman wearing a silver dress that she'd no doubt had to be poured into sauntered over to me.

She stood at my elbow, close enough that her titties brushed against my arm with every inhalation—way closer than was acceptable since we didn't know each other—and ran a finger down my arm. Nothing but bad vibes wafted off of her, and I glanced around the room, wondering how much longer Monie was going to be.

"I don't want to be disrespectful to your…*friend* or whatever, but I just had to come over here and tell you how muthafuckin' fine you are."

The woman licked her lips, eyes roving me from head to toe much like Director Timms' ten minutes earlier, likely thinking that she'd just caught me with that unimaginative ass line issued in that forced sultry voice, but all I could do was burst out laughing.

"How the fuck are you gon' say you don't wanna be disrespectful, but then—in the same breath—say some *wildly* disrespectful shit? How that work, lil mama?" Sipping my drink, I quirked an eyebrow at her as I waited for her excuse. Something told me that she had one.

She shrugged like it was no big deal and shifted her weight so that the high slit in the center of her dress parted to reveal two caramel thighs. I glanced down at them and let my eyes take a slow journey up her body until I reached her artfully made-up face and bone-straight red hair. She smirked at me, obviously knowing that she looked good, and proud that I noticed. Yeah, she was sexy, but this shit right here was ugly as fuck. I shook my head and chuckled. *Some women were so damn trifling.* Aisha, Lisette, and Monie said it often, but it was always a shock to experience it in real-time.

"They say a closed mouth don't get fed so…"

Trifling as fuck.

Laughing, I moved an inch to my right. "And you think you're 'gon eat when I arrived at this event on somebody else's plate?"

Waving her hand in the air like she was fanning

away my words, she pursed her lips and propped her other hand on her hip.

"She's never posted you, so I figured you were fair game."

Behind this random, thirsty-ass woman's head, I could see Monie approaching us and I smiled. That fucking dress was turning heads all around the room and had my damn heart beating a little bit faster. Monie was bad as fuck and she knew that shit, each step commanding attention, her enviable curves making mouths water. Without taking my eyes off of her, I gave the woman an answer to the slick question she was trying to ask.

"I'm not."

Even if Monie and I weren't making our way toward being together, I would never embarrass her by fucking with one of her fans—and this woman was obviously a fan if she'd stalked enough of Monie's posts to know that she'd never posted me.

Monie brushed past the woman and circled behind me before coming to stand on my left, the action causing a cloud of her perfume-scented air to waft over my face. It was something about that scent that made my stomach clench.

"Hey y'all," Monie greeted amicably.

The woman—whose name I still didn't know—

smiled broadly. "Hi, Monelle! You look amazing, and that beat is superb!"

"Thanks, hun," replied Monie with a gracious tilt of her head.

I smirked. I *knew* the damn woman was a fan. No one who knew Mo personally called her by her whole name. Since we'd been at the event it'd been "Monelle" this and "Monelle" that. I'd only noticed two people calling her Monie. Placing my hand at the small of her back, I turned to Mo. Her eyes weren't as bright, and her smile was drooping at the corners. She looked tired, and with good reason. We'd been at the event for four hours, and except for the forty-five-minute break for dinner and the awards, she'd been constantly moving around the room, playing the professional game by networking.

Leaning in so that I was speaking directly into her ear, I asked, "You ready to go?"

She looked at me, looked at the woman, who had walked off and was now talking to someone else, and then looked at me again. Her face was impassive, but there was something in her eyes that I couldn't decipher. After a moment she nodded.

"Yeah, let's go."

We walked back to our table to retrieve her award and made our way to the door. Several people stopped us to congratulate Monie on her win, but eventually we exited the building and were in my car heading to Monie's place. After about ten minutes of riding quietly with the radio low and set to Majic 102.1, letting the Quiet Storm help us wind down from the excitement of the night, Monie turned to me, her lips twisted with a full attitude.

"You kind of rushed me out of there. Tryna hurry up and drop me off so you can meet up with ole girl for a smash and dash?"

That shit had come out of left field, completely pulling me out of my thoughts of how good Monie smelled and why that fucking perfume had my stomach rumbling as if I hadn't eaten a steak fit for a king at the event. Frowning, I shot a quick glance her way before returning my eyes to the road.

"What?"

Rolling her eyes, she tilted her head. "Which part didn't you understand?"

"All of it, but you can start by explaining how I *rushed you out of there*' when we'd been there for hours. You looked tired, so I asked if you were ready. How is that '*rushing*' you?"

Eyes narrowed, she glared at me and sucked her teeth. "Whatever! I see you're conveniently ignoring the other part of what I said."

Laughing, I navigated my car down the exit ramp that would take me to Monie's townhouse in the east end. "I don't even know who that woman is, Mo."

"Does that even matter?"

In truth, it didn't, not if I was trying to do what she was accusing me of, but saying that would only exacerbate whatever it was that had her on ten.

"What did the director want to talk to you about?"

Her eyes narrowed. "Wow. You're just going to change the subject.

"Man," I drawled, shifting my left hand to the top of the steering wheel and using my right to cup the back of her neck, "you're trying to make something an issue that wasn't even on my radar and I'm not feeling it. I know you liken me to a puppy, but I promise you, I'm not that easily distracted."

The car fell quiet as she glared at me. Then she pursed her lips and snatched her head away from my hand. "Fuck you."

Her eyes were tight, and her lips were curled in obvious anger. She was big mad and I couldn't help but laugh.

"Why are you mad at me, Mo? I didn't even do anything to you."

I watched as she folded her arms and twisted her body away from me, staring out the window.

"*That's the fucking problem*," she gritted in a tone so low that I almost missed it.

And wait—what?!

Knowing that she didn't say what I thought I'd heard, I asked, "What'd you just say?"

But she didn't say anything.

"Monie, I know damn well your ass isn't ignoring me."

Still nothing.

I was generally a pretty easygoing dude. I laughed and joked more than the average, but I had a big heart and a lot of love for my people. There were few things on earth with the power to tank my mood or make me blow up. Unfortunately, one of those things was being ignored. With as many years as our friendship spanned, Monie definitely knew that shit, which meant she was trying to piss me off on purpose.

But why?

FOUR

BEDROOM BOOM

I'd barely shifted the gears into park before Monie was climbing out of my car and stalking up the sidewalk to her gate. All I could do was shake my head at her dramatics. Reaching into the backseat, I grabbed her forgotten award and then quickly hopped out of my car, using my remote to lock the doors as I jogged up behind her. Catching the gate just before it swung closed in my face, I shouldered the heavy barrier back open and took a moment to steady my footing and dust off the arms of my tuxedo jacket before continuing up the walk-way that led to her door. She was already inside, and the door was closed, but when I tried the knob, it turned easily in my hand. I chuckled, Monie might have been pissed, but at least she wasn't literally locking me out.

Stepping inside her cool apartment, I locked the door behind me and followed the sound of glass clinking. I found Monie in the kitchen, leaning against the counter as she poured a generous glass of dark red wine. Setting the heavy award on the counter, I watched as she drained the glass in one go before licking her plump lips and immediately refilling it, bringing it to her mouth once more.

"Shit, Mo. I thought you had a good night, but you're sucking down that wine like they got up on that stage and said your makeup looks like you graduated from clown college."

Cutting her eyes at me, she lowered the glass and licked her lips. I was momentarily distracted by the lack of a lipstick stain on the glass in her hand.

"I'm good, Vick. You can go now."

There was a hard edge to her voice that let me know she was the exact opposite of good. So, instead of leaving, I walked up to her and hugged her from behind. Wrapping my arms around her waist, I settled my chin on her shoulder and pressed my cheek against hers. When a disgusted sound burst from her throat, I rubbed my face against hers and squeezed her tighter, using a child-like tone when I said, "Aww, Mo. What'sa matter with da baaaabyyy?"

Groaning, she tried to jerk her head away from

me. "Ugh, Vick, get the fuck off of me! You're gonna mess up my beat!"

Sucking my teeth, I ignored her screeching and buried my face in her neck. "You already know I don't give a shit about this makeup, girl. Tell me the truth."

My actions were doing the double duty of working to annoy her with my proximity and give me an opportunity to have her in my arms while I inhaled more of that perfume that had my heart doing somersaults in my chest.

With my hands splayed across her stomach, I felt her release a heavy sigh. "Since you won't let this go…the truth is that I'm lonely. Everybody has somebody but me. Darwin has Carrie; Shad and Aisha have each other; hell, even Lisette has a secret boo that she's keeping under wraps."

I waited for her to continue, and when she didn't, I poked her in the side, trying hard to act like the little gasp and giggle she released didn't thrill me.

"How are you gon' say 'everybody' but leave me out? I ain't nobody, Mo?" I ignored the admission that she was lonely since I was ready and willing to put an end to that.

She sighed again and brought her glass to her lips for a significantly smaller sip of wine. Bending her right leg, she shifted her weight from one foot to the other. The move lifted her ass and pressed it right against my crotch. I held my breath, waiting for her to realize what she'd done and move away or even say something, but she didn't.

Maybe I was tripping.

Maybe I imagined the contact.

The clink of her glass hitting the countertop brought my attention back to her just in time to hear her say some rude—and false—shit.

"Oh, please. Everybody knows you don't do relationships. You *talk*, that's it."

Tilting my head, I eyed her. "Yo, that's a flagrant lie! I don't do relationships with the wrong people. And I definitely do more than talk."

She pursed her lips, instantly drawing my eyes to her mouth. The glossy, nude lipstick that she'd worn had managed to hang around all night, and I wondered what else it could withstand since it had made it through dinner and several glasses of wine.

"Yeah, fool. I'm quite sure you do more than talk. You *definitely* out here fucking too."

Grinning, I shrugged. "Not as much as the consensus seems to have agreed on, but a little bit, yeah."

She cocked her head and shot me a disbelieving look. Slowly, I trailed my contemplative gaze from her mouth to her eyes, which were outlined in thick black lines, dusted with silver glitter on her lids, and framed by long lashes. For a moment, we just stared at each other in silence; her eyes narrowed in confusion while my own showed everything I'd been holding on to for entirely too long. After a beat, she sucked in a breath and snapped her head forward, staring down at her now empty glass on the counter.

"Um…" I could sense her indecision as well as if it were sitting on the counter. Finally, she asked, "What's a little bit, Vick?"

There was something important about her asking me that question. I could feel it in my gut. "Before or after I started saving myself for you."

She sucked in a breath, and I chuckled into her neck.

"Mo."

With her eyes still trained on her glass, she asked, "Huh?"

Running my nose along the long line of her neck, relishing in the shiver I elicited, I murmured, "Ask me."

"Vick…" Her tone was pleading, something I couldn't remember ever hearing from her, but now that I had, I wanted to again, and in a different capacity.

"*Ask. Me.*"

It was so quiet in her apartment that I heard the click of her throat as she swallowed. "When?"

"At least a year. Easy."

"Why?"

"Why what, Mo?"

"Why has it been a year? What have you been waiting for?"

Finally! I smirked and pressed a soft kiss to the exposed skin on her shoulder. The way her fingers tightened around the stem of her wine glass giving me the go-ahead to lay it all out. "I've been waiting for you to stop playing."

She dropped her head forward, and I took the opportunity to sweep her hair over her shoulder and kiss the back of her neck.

"This isn't funny, Vick," she whined.

Trailing my fingers down her back, I once again wrapped my arms around her, resuming my position and pressing my chest against her back.

"Does it sound like I'm joking, Mo? Are you honestly gon' stand here and try to pretend that something hasn't been brewing between us over the past few months?"

For a beat, she didn't say anything, and I felt a stab of fear that she might try and do just that, but then she surprised me by turning in my arms and grabbing me by the lapels, yanking me toward her until our lips were inches apart.

"As tempted as I am to tear your ass up—and believe me, I am incredibly tempted—you're not big enough to ride this ride."

Offended, I jerked back, pulling out of her grasp. This was the second time that she'd said that shit, and it was imperative that I dead that immediately. "Not big enough?! Girl, you know damn well you felt this anaconda on your ass just now!"

Biting her lip, she dropped her eyes to my crotch, and I saw the curiosity in her eyes before it morphed into mirth. "Garden snake, maybe, but that's not the point. I'm not talking about the size of your dick, Vick. What do you weigh? A buck fifty?"

Laughing, I shook my head. She was buggin'.

"C'mon man. Why are you tryna play me right now? What does my weight have to do with anything?"

Monie slid to the side and posed, running a hand from her chest to her thigh. "It matters because what you see in front of you is a full-grown woman, and I'll be damned if I let *another* nigga get between my legs, only for him to try and make me feel like shit because *he* bit off more than he could chew. Now, I'll ask you one—"

Over all of the rah-rah she was talking, I stepped

up to her and bent my knees slightly, wrapping my arms under her ass. Straightening, I lifted her into the air and pivoted to sit her on the counter.

"You done?" I asked, beyond ready to be the next nigga between her legs.

Lips parted and jaw loose, she regarded me dazedly. All I could do was chuckle. Squeezing her calves, I ducked my head to catch her unfocused gape.

"Mo," I called. "Are. You. Done?"

Her mouth didn't move, but her eyes—wide and filled with equal measures of trepidation and lust—said everything I needed to hear. Digging my fingers into her thighs, I pulled her closer to the edge of the counter. She widened her knees, giving me more room to step between them and enter her personal space. I leaned toward her, pleased when I saw her coming my way as well, but inches before our mouths met, I halted. If she wouldn't give me a verbal answer to my question, she couldn't get my lips—or any other body part—on her.

Noticing how my momentum had stopped, Monie's brows furrowed in confusion for the briefest of seconds, then her eyes narrowed and she grabbed the lapels of my tuxedo, yanking me toward her.

"Don't fucking play with me," she gritted, slanting her head and connecting her full lips to mine.

While it wasn't exactly "I want you, Vick," it would work—for now. Sliding my hands underneath the slit of her dress, I ran my palms along the supple skin of her smooth thighs until I reached the dips where her pelvis began. The barely-there scalloped edge of her lace panties brushed my knuckles, and I dipped the tips of my fingers underneath the fabric, swallowing Monie's resultant moan into my mouth. She tasted so good—felt so good against me—that I could have stood there in that kitchen and kissed her forever.

Apparently, Monie had other plans. She wrapped her legs around my back and scooted forward, pulling me even closer until I could feel the heat from her pussy against my abdomen. Locking her feet together at the ankles, she pressed them against my lower back, using them as leverage while she ground against me. Her obvious desire had my dick hard as fuck, and I trailed my hands over her hips to grip her ass and pull her flush against me, all the while, sucking her tongue into my mouth as she dug her nails into my shoulders. The need for air was the only thing that made me sever our connection. I pulled back, chest heaving hard as I stared at her. Her eyes fluttered open, the thick lashes making them appear larger and rounder than usual.

"Tell me what you want, Mo."

Her lips parted and she blew out a soft, silent breath. "I want us to move this into my bedroom."

My dick throbbed at the thought, and I squeezed her ass. "And what do you want to happen once we're in there?"

"Fucking. So much fucking."

Licking my lips, I nodded. I wanted that too, but I also wanted so much more from her. "Done. And after that?"

Her curls bounced as she shook her head. "I don't know. We can cross that bridge once we get to it."

"Mo—" That sure as hell wasn't what I wanted to hear.

"No, Vick," she interrupted. "Right now, the only thing I'm thinking about is getting filled like a Christmas stocking by that garden snake in your pants. Anything else is background noise."

"Anaconda," I instantly corrected. "Oh, so you want my candy cane and sugar plums, huh?"

She rolled her eyes, trying to fight a grin, but failing beautifully. "Yeah, Vick. I want it all, brand new socks and draws."

Tossing my head back, I howled with laughter. "Aight, bet."

Sliding my hands into the folds of her dress, I gripped her hips and pulled her to the edge of the counter. She tightened her legs around my waist and wrapped her arms around my neck.

"You'd better not drop me, Vick!"

Chuckling, I lifted her into my arms and carried her into her bedroom.

"Yeah, yeah. I hear you, but if I dropped you on this dick, you wouldn't have shit to say."

I waited on a comeback or smart retort, but she just shuddered in my arms and pressed her chest closer to mine. In her room, I flipped the switch by the door, bathing the room in a muted yellow light. Monie's room was decorated in shades of pink and gray, with strings of twinkling lights decorating the wall behind her bed and twisted around the frame of the canopy. There were large pieces of art stretched across four canvases covering two walls, and in one corner of the room was a vanity and matching chair next to a five-foot chest of draws with the top covered in makeup.

I sat Monie on the bed and leaned down to kiss her. Her lips parted and her tongue darted out to meet mine, pulling a groan out of me. Bringing her hands to my waist, she dug her fingers into me before pulling away, ending the kiss just before it really got started. Her breathing was a little labored as she stared up at me.

"What's up?" I questioned.

"Just..." she licked her lips. "Wait a minute. Let me go remove my makeup."

I took a step back, giving her room as she scrambled off of the bed and rushed into the bathroom, closing and locking the door behind her. Turning, I sat in the spot she'd just abandoned and bent to remove my shoes. My eyes landed on the plush rug and I smirked. It was wild that I was here right now. As much as I wanted Monie, I wasn't sure that she'd give me a chance, and if she did, at least not so quickly. It seemed like only days had passed since we shared that kiss on New Year's, so to be in her bedroom, about to lay pipe as if my nickname was Luigi, was a wonder.

The bathroom door opened, pulling me out of my thoughts and bringing my attention across the room. Monie appeared in the doorway wearing a sheer, floor-length robe that displayed every curve, dip, and divot. Desire for her swelled inside of me and my eyes narrowed, stuttering over the dark circles of her areolas as I surveyed her body. Observing her nudity felt like staring at the works of art on the walls.

I realized then that I'd been in my head longer than I'd thought, and hadn't taken the opportunity to get undressed while she was in the bathroom. While Monie stood across the room looking like every one of my fantasies, I still wore my tuxedo. Standing to my feet, I loosened my tie and started to undo my cuff links when Monie strutted toward me and grabbed my wrists.

"All night, I thought of stripping you out of this tuxedo. Please, let me fulfill that fantasy."

Both my heart and my dick swelled. *What words could I possibly say after hearing her admission?* There were none, so I nodded and dropped my hands to my side. With deft fingers, Monie plucked my cuff links out of my shirt and jacket, and then slipped off my tie as she pushed my jacket off of my shoulders.

"Do you know how fucking sexy you are?" she murmured as she reached around me to release my cummerbund, dropping the fabric onto the floor and unbuttoning the crisp white shirt beneath it. It almost sounded like a rhetorical question, as if she was speaking to herself and I was eavesdropping.

"Beautiful, peanut-butter brown skin," she continued, trailing her fingers over my shoulder blades as she removed my shirt, "sharp cheekbones and strong jawline," her fingers danced a feather-light routine over each bit of skin that she referenced, causing a ripple of full-body shivers to travel through my body.

My chest tightened, face warm from her observation, not at all expecting to feel so...revered. Of course, I knew what I looked like. I knew that plenty of women cataloged my features and found me attractive, but knowing that Monie was one of those women set my body ablaze. The one woman I wanted more than my next breath saw me as someone to be desired and admired, and not just as her friend who she didn't notice because of one reason or another. It was one boulder of a roadblock on the journey to making her mine that was removed without me having to lift a finger.

She continued detailing my characteristics as she undressed me until I was standing before her wearing nothing but my watch and the simple gold chain that I never removed. Monie had even pulled off my dress socks and complimented my toes in a move that almost had me pulling a Shad and dropping onto one knee while declaring my love for her right then. While it would have been true, I had more work to do to get her comfortable with us morphing into an *us*. I was more than willing to put in the work, starting with fucking her so good that she wouldn't even be able to look at me without her pussy quaking.

Pressing her hands to my chest, Monie shoved me backward, making me fall to a seated position at the edge of her bed. Eyes heavy with anticipation, I watched as she walked around me and grabbed one of the decorative pillows off of her bed and dropped it between my feet before gripping each of my knees and lowering herself between them. Reaching into the fur-lined sleeve of her robe, Monie retrieved an elastic band and swept her hair up into a bun on top of her head. My eyes grew to saucers as I realized what she was about to do.

Kneeling between my legs, she looked up at me, bare face unable to hide anything, and wide eyes telling me everything. It was evident in the way that her lids were weighed down by lust that she wanted this just as much as I did, but there was something else swirling in those chocolate depths that I couldn't deny.

She was terrified.

It was right there, front and center, and I wracked my brain trying to think of ways to reassure her. She needed to know there was nothing to be afraid of with me; that I would take care of her heart as if it was sitting inside of my own chest.

"We won't let this change things, right?" Her voice was soft but insistent as she searched my face for an answer.

With knitted brows, I stared down at her and cycled through potential responses, searching for the words that wouldn't ruin the mood by inciting an argument. The one question bouncing around in my brain made it difficult.

Had I not been clear with my intentions?

"Mo," I husked, "I'm hoping that this changes *everything* between us."

Shock arrested her features, widening her eyes and loosening her jaw until her parted lips formed an "o". Leaning back, she shook her head.

"Why would you say that?"

She sounded truly distressed, which only worked to deepen my frown. *Had she not heard a word I'd said to her before we made our way to her bedroom? Or hell, was she even listening to what I'd said to her before we kissed the first time? Seriously?*

Bending forward, I cupped her face in my hands, hoping that the vital eye contact displayed the sincerity that I felt down to my core.

"Because it's true. I mean, yeah, I wanna fuck you with every fiber of my being right now, but I also want to love you with everything that's in me *and* everything that isn't. I just need you to want me too and let me do that shit."

Seemingly speechless, she stared back at me, her fingers digging into my thighs as her eyes glossed over. Hope swelled in my chest when she parted her lips to speak, but then she blinked rapidly and whatever I thought I'd seen brewing in her face disappeared like rainclouds after a storm. Shaking her head, she knocked my hands from her face and dropped her leer to my uncovered dick.

Releasing my knees, she took me into her warm hands and began to stroke me from base to tip in a loose hold.

Dragging my hands down my face, I groaned. "Fuck, Mo. You don't play fair."

"Not if I can help it," she murmured. Her grin was wicked and sexy as fuck. Opening her mouth, she displayed her wide, pink tongue before swirling it around the head of my dick.

"Shit!" I yelped the moment she took me into her mouth.

She didn't give me any time to adjust or prepare, swallowing me down completely and sparking up a rhythm that had my hips bucking within minutes. My fingers gripped the sheets so tightly that I was sure my knuckles would be sore the next day. After flexing them for probably the tenth time, Monie once again shocked the shit out of me by grabbing my hands and placing them at the back of her head—without pulling her mouth from my dick.

I didn't hesitate to dig my fingers into her thick hair, purposefully mussing the loose bun she'd created, excited to have been granted permission to not only touch her hair but grip it tightly. The moment my fingers connected with her scalp she went into hyperdrive, jerking me and sucking me with a single-minded focus that had me groaning her name on the tail-end of a curse as I shot my release into the back of her throat.

Chest heaving, I watched as she sat back and wiped at the corners of her mouth with the tips of her ring fingers before smirking at me. Licking my lips, I swallowed hard.

"If you were tryna convince me that I shouldn't love you, that was the wrong way to go about it. Now I'm 'bout to go buy a ring."

Her face brightened as she leaned her head back and laughed, displaying all her teeth, her empty mouth, and the long column of her neck. I just stared at her, only half-joking.

"Didn't you say you'd have me climbing the walls?" Canting her head to the side, she splayed her hands on her thighs. "I'm feeling a little hoodwinked. Nay, bamboozled!" Having sucked a nut out of me, she was feeling victorious and playful, but I was ready to move forward.

"Bring your ass up on this bed," I commanded.

Her laughter faded out, and when our eyes met, the heat in those molten chocolate irises made my dick throb and jump of its own volition. Sitting forward, I helped her onto her feet and then undid the knotted belt at her waist. The robe fell open and I sucked my bottom lip between my teeth to prevent me from drooling at the sight in front of me. Every inch of Monie's body was perfection dipped in cocoa, and I wanted—*needed*—to devour every last drop.

Lifting my eyes to hers, I realized at that moment that I suddenly understood exactly what TLC meant, because I for damn sure wasn't too proud to beg for what stood before me. Gliding my hands over her belly and around her hips to grip her ass, I tugged her toward me.

"Can I have this, Mo? Please?"

Instantly, she gave me a slow shake of her head as she pulled my hands from her ass and guided them up to her heavy breasts, where my thumbs immediately sought out her tight nipples.

"No," she murmured, "but you can play with it for the night."

I didn't get the opportunity to protest because she cupped my chin and brought her lips to mine. She leaned into me and I scooted backward on the bed, taking care not to break our connection. Following me to the center of the mattress, Monie parted her lips and accepted my tongue, sucking it into her mouth as I massaged her breasts and tugged on her nipples. Lying back, I grabbed her hips and pulled her on top of me, settling her knees on either side of my body.

While holding her in place with one hand, I slid the other between our bodies, traveling south until my fingers met the damp flesh at the juncture of her thighs. She gasped into my mouth as I ran my fingers up and down her wet slit, and she almost bit my damn tongue off when I slid two fingers inside of her and began thrusting. Opening my eyes, I watched her face as I fucked her. She broke our kiss and dropped her head back, rocking against my hand, rubbing her clit against my palm as she clutched my shoulders tightly. Leaning forward, I peppered kisses along her neck before sucking one of her nipples into my mouth at the same time that I began swiping my thumb along her clit in brisk strokes.

Monie's face contorted as she rode my hand, and I watched in awe as she came in a wet gush, crying out in a jumble of words that I didn't understand but could wholeheartedly agree with. As her pussy throbbed around my fingers, I slid my arm around her waist to keep her in place while I sped up my thrusts and increased the pressure on her clit, kissing up the valley of her breasts.

"Wha—*wait!*" she moaned. "Vick. *Wait.*"

I shook my head and slid a third finger into her. "Nah. You said I could play with it, so I'mma play with it."

This orgasm hit her faster than the first and

seemed to last longer, with me continuously fucking her through it. I was primed and ready to go for a third when she scrambled out of my grasp, whimpering when my fingers fell from her slick heat.

"Whatchu doin'?" I asked, blinking lazily and biting my lip as I watched her roll to the edge of the bed and stumble toward the nightstand.

Instead of answering me, she held up a handful of condoms and a bottle of lube. Tossing the condoms my way, she gripped the lube and climbed back onto the bed, crawling toward me with her eyes trained on my face. Understanding brought a smile to my face. I beheld her as she approached me, refusing to look away even as I brought my hand to my mouth to lick and suck the evidence of her pleasure from each digit.

When she settled between my legs, I started to reach for her, but she swatted my hand away and rolled the condom down over my dick. My stomach concaved as she squirted a generous amount of lube and slowly jerked me to distribute the gel, before crawling over me and pressing another scorching kiss to my lips. Pushing up into the kiss, I brought my hands to her hips and helped guide her as she sank onto me. Twin groans filled the air and Monie dropped her head onto my shoulder as continued lowering herself until I was fully seated inside of her.

"Shit, Mo," I murmured, fingers digging into the flesh of her ass. "You feel so fucking good, baby." Her wet warmth felt like the most comforting hug I'd ever been privileged to receive. It was the perfect fit, her soaked walls massaging my dick with every pulse, and I already knew it would be hard for me to climb out of her when this was through.

Although she let out a series of soft grunts, Monie didn't say a word. She sat up, planted her hands on either side of my head, and started slapping her big ass on me.

"Fuck!"

The way she swallowed and released me was havoc on my senses. Looping my arms around her waist, I crossed my arms at the elbow and gripped her cheeks. I wasn't trying to control her rhythm; I just needed to hang on for dear life. Just when I thought I was getting a handle on my emotions, she switched it up. She went from pounding my shit to winding her hips in tight circles, grinding down onto my dick tortuously slowly.

Squeezing my eyes shut, I pressed my head into the mattress, desperately trying to keep from shedding a tear. Monie was blowing my fucking mind and I was helpless to stop it—not that I wanted to. When she sped up the winding of her hips and started rocking into me, I began to feel that familiar stirring in my body that let me know my release was imminent.

Desperately, I brought my hand right back to her clit, hoping to slow her down with another orgasm, but my idea backfired. As she came again, her pussy clamped down on me, immediately wrenching my nut from me in the blink of an eye. I thrust up into her, grabbed her bun, and pulled her mouth to mine for a savage kiss as we rode out the rest of our release in tandem. Eventually, Monie collapsed against me, and I tightened my arms around her, not wanting to lose her warmth or the feel of her softness against me.

When her breathing slowed, she lifted her head and peered down at me. The band in her hair was literally hanging on by a thread, and her face was flushed and damp with sweat. Her eyes were wide, irises blown out. She looked thoroughly fucked and beautiful as hell.

"Are you staying the night?"

Trailing my fingers over her lips, I nodded. "I'm not going anywhere until you put me out."

Grinning, she leaned forward and pressed a chaste kiss to my jawline.

"Good."

FIVE
BEFORE DINNER MINTS

onie's schedule was booked solid in the weeks following the event. During the day, she would work on the television show, but after she won her award, her calendar for her mobile makeup business exploded. No one in the crew saw her thanks to a destination wedding one weekend and appointment after appointment. I respected her grind and didn't complain, although I desperately wanted to see her. Mercifully, she answered when I called her at night, blessing me with her voice and phone sex a couple of those nights. It was nothing compared to seeing her though, so when she finally got a moment to breathe, I invited her out to spend a little time with me and have some fun.

Arriving at her place more than an hour before the time I'd instructed her to be ready, I handed her two wrapped packages and stepped inside of her living room, closing and locking the door behind me. As she stood there, staring down at the pink boxes, I lifted her chin to drop a kiss on her lips and made my way over to the sofa. It wasn't until I sat down that Monie looked up from her gifts and found my eyes.

"Vick…what's this?"

"Open 'em and see."

I laughed as she shook her head.

"Why not?"

Crossing the room, she sat on the ottoman and rested the packages on her knees.

"Just tell me," she whined.

I was shaking my head before she even finished her sentence.

"Stop bein' a punk and open the damn boxes."

Shooting me a glare, she flipped me the bird as she set the larger box on the floor by her feet and brought the smaller one to her ear before giving it a shake. It was like Christmas all over again as an uncontrollable grin tugged her lips upward. Ripping at the glittery paper, it didn't take her long to reveal the black shoe box inside, and the moment that she noticed the logo, Monie's eyes jerked up to me.

"What is this, Vick?"

"Man. Open it."

She narrowed her eyes at me, but I gave her a silly

look and bit my lip, not saying another word. Realizing that I wasn't going to give her an answer, Monie turned back to the box in her lap and lifted the lid. Slowly, her lips curved into a surprised smile, and I expected her to look at me and ask me once again what it was that she was looking at, but instead, she set the box on the floor and picked up the larger box. This time, she took her time removing the wrapping from this box, running her hands over the paper, probably taking in the slight bumps and grooves of the embossing. Once unwrapped, she lifted the white lid and set it on the floor next to the first box. Her brows furrowed, and she shot me a bewildered glance.

There were no words this time, she just turned back to the box and lifted its contents into the air. It was a long-sleeved jumpsuit in the same ice blue color as the dress she'd worn to the event. It also matched the sneakers in the box that she'd already set on the floor, as well as the shirt that I had on underneath my hoodie, and the identical pair of sneakers on my feet.

Laying the garment across her legs, Monie turned to me.

"Now that I have this open if I ask you what this is, will you tell me?"

Smirking, I tilted my head to the side. "Now that

you have it open, is it really necessary for you to ask me what it is?"

Monie rolled her eyes. "Do you have to be so damn difficult all of the time?"

I shook my head. "Nah. Not all the time. Just… About seventy-five percent of the time."

Head tilted, she studied me. "It's funny. I never would have pegged you for a matchy-matchy type of dude."

It was too damn easy, but I never claimed that to be a problem for me. Cheesing hard as a muthafucka, I held her gaze with my own. "You can peg me however you'd like, Mo. I told you, it's yours for the taking."

Her eyes widened and she began blinking rapidly. Chuckling, I gave her a lifeline. "I know it's gonna take you a minute to finish getting ready, since you gotta match your makeup to your fit, so go ahead and get dressed. I'mma chill out here and wait for you."

She stared at me with an indecipherable look in her eyes, then she licked her lips and sat forward.

"So…you want me to wear this?"

"Yeah. The moment I saw it, all I could think about was how good it would look on your body, so I bought it." I shrugged. "But if you don't want to wear it, I'll understand." Nodding toward the opened box on the floor, I added, "You gotta rock the shoes though."

She looked down at the opened box near her bare toes, took in the shoes, and then twisted on the ottoman to observe my feet. When she lifted her chin, that confused look was still on her face, and it annoyed the fuck out of me. *What was there to be confused about?* I waited to see if she would ask the question that was so evident in her eyes, but instead of saying anything else, she gathered up the jumpsuit and snatched up the shoes into her hand, and walked into her bedroom.

When her door closed behind her, I gathered up the wrapping paper and the empty boxes and put them into the garbage. I pulled the full bag out of the garbage can, tied it up, and ran it out to the dumpster. Stepping back into her apartment, I washed my hands and put a new bag inside of the empty can before dropping down onto the couch and pulling out my phone. However, as soon as the device was in my hand, the nagging in my brain refused to let me chill. The look on Monie's face before she went into her room kept flashing in my mind, and I realized that I had to get something straight before we went further with the night.

Back on my feet, I rapped lightly on her door with the side of my knuckle. Pressing my ear to the door, I listened but didn't hear anything, so I turned the knob and walked inside. Just as I was stepping into her bedroom, Monie opened the door of her bathroom. We met eyes for a moment, but then I gave her a lingering once over. She'd obviously been in the middle of getting dressed because all she wore was a bra that had her titties sitting right up underneath her chin and a pair of skimpy black panties. Groaning, I bit my lip. The woman was a masterpiece.

Noticing how my expression had changed, Monie folded her arms under her breasts, quirked an eyebrow, and leaned against the door jamb.

"Uh, can I help you?"

Licking my lips and closing the door behind me, I stalked toward her slowly.

"Yeah, actually, you can. You can help me by letting go of whatever this is that has you thinking that I'm not here for the reason that I've repeatedly given you."

Frowning, she propped her hands on her wide hips. "What the hell are you talking about, Vick? At least let me go in the closet and get my damn thinking cap if you're gonna be talking in riddles."

Standing in front of her, I bent my knees and looped my arms around her thighs, lifting her into my arms. Immediately, she wrapped her arms around my neck, holding on tight while I carried her over to the bed and set her down. Her knees were on either side of my body, as she dropped her hands to the bed on either side of her, clutching the duvet in her fingers.

It was imperative that she understood this wasn't a joke for me, so I wiped all traces of a smile from my face. Peering down at her intently, I waited for her eyes to meet mine, tamping down a smirk when she quirked an eyebrow at me.

"We're going on a date, Monie. This isn't some extension-of-the-crew type of hanging out; this is romance. We're going on a date because I want to be your man and you need to get used to spending time with me outside of the crew. Is that understood?"

After my little declaration, I stared down at her, waiting for her response, expecting some smart ass remark, but she shocked the fuck out of me by not saying anything at all and simply nodding. Since her silence was better than her shutting me down, I smiled, leaned down to press a quick kiss to her lips, and started to back up out of her space so that I could leave her room and let her finish getting dressed. I'd barely gotten two steps away from her when she grabbed my belt. Curious, I met her eyes, and the heated look in those dark brown depths finished the job that seeing her barely clothed had started. My dick was steadily rising, but we had somewhere to be, so I willed it to go down.

"What's up?" I asked, not allowing myself to be pulled back toward her or that bed that looked as soft as I remembered.

"You can't talk to me like that and then walk out of here like everything's all regular," she announced in a sultry voice.

At that point, my smirk was impossible to contain, and I had to link my hands behind my head to keep from touching her. If I touched her, we weren't leaving the room for a while.

"How did I talk to you?"

"All authoritative and shit," she damn near moaned. "Like you're running something around here, and I'm just 'posed to say '*Yes sir, Daddy*'."

She spread her legs and reached between them to pull the crotch of her panties to the side, revealing an already glistening set of fat lips. With her other hand, she released my belt and cupped my rock-hard dick through my pants, squeezing with just enough pressure to make my hips jerk forward.

Dropping my head back, I groaned and squeezed my eyes shut. "We got somewhere to be, Mo. We don't have time for this right now." There wasn't only a *note* of pleading in my voice, it was a whole ass composition tap-dancing on my vocal cords.

Monie squeezed my dick again, making my eyes fly open as I looked at her just in time to see her raise an eyebrow at me. "It doesn't feel like he agrees with you. It seems like he's on my side—like he wants to be *in* my insides."

"Shit," I muttered in a strained voice, not even in a position to point out how corny that was because it was true as fuck.

The brain in my pants wasn't the only one that wanted to be inside of Monie. But we truly didn't have time for that. So, I did the only thing I could do. I dropped to my knees, dragged Monie's panties down to the middle of her thighs, lifted her thick legs into the air, and dove my face into her pussy. I slurped at her folds for a few seconds before sucking her clit into my mouth and rubbing two fingers through her wetness. Once they were good and wet, I slid those two digits inside of her, finger-fucking her at a steady pace while flicking my tongue up and down her pink pearl until she was cursing me out in two different languages and tugging on my ears as she came.

As soon as her cries began to taper out, I jumped to my feet and backed toward the door, eyes trained on her face, which was still contorted in ecstasy. The desire to feel the aftershocks of her orgasm on my dick was so intense that I needed to get out of the room immediately or we'd never make it out of her house.

Mo lowered her feet to the floor and gave me a look so heated I was liable to burst into flames. My dick throbbed, and I shook my head.

"Vick—" she all but moaned, but I cut her off with a shake of my head.

"I'm going for a short walk. Please be ready to go by the time I get back."

Without waiting for an answer, I spun on my heels and hurried out onto the sidewalk. It took two spins around her complex before I managed to talk my dick down off the ledge. He was ready to dive head-first right into her pussy and didn't want to hear a thing about building a foundation outside of the bedroom. When I reentered Monie's townhouse, she was on the couch, looking down at her phone. I sent up a silent prayer of thanks and hovered near the door.

"You ready?"

She looked up from her device and stood, a smirk etched on her lips. Lifting the thin strap of a small bag over her neck, she sauntered toward me.

"You know that you owe me a debt, right?"

Giving her a once-over, I marveled at how well the jumpsuit fit her. Peeling her out of it was going to be like unwrapping a present of my own. When my eyes met hers, I grinned.

"Is that right?" We stepped outside and I waited while she locked the door. "What's my balance?"

"At least two dicks and one mouth."

Opening the passenger door, I laughed as she climbed inside. Once I settled behind the wheel, I eyed her.

"How did I manage to get so behind? I could've sworn I was on auto-pay."

She shrugged. "I don't know what you've been doing with your funds. That mouth you just paid was nice, but I want all of my things, and I want them asaptually."

With my hand behind her seat, I backed out of my parking space and pulled out onto the street.

"Well shit. I'll be sure to take care of that before the night is over. Can't have debt like that hanging over my head."

Monie nodded, giving me a playful smile before looking out of the window. "As long as you know."

SIX

DATE NIGHT

The jumpsuit fit Monie like a fucking glove. I couldn't decide if it was a good thing or a bad thing. On one hand, witnessing her strut into the raceway with her titties sitting, hips swinging, and head high was a sight to see. I was proud as fuck and having a hard time taking my eyes off of her. But on the other hand, *I was having a hard fucking time taking my eyes off of her*. It wouldn't have been an issue except I kept crashing my go-kart into the barriers because every few seconds I couldn't help but search for her in the crowd of eight drivers as we repeatedly raced through the winding course.

We'd chosen the outside course. It was loud as hell, but I was so tuned into Monie that I could hear her peals of laughter over the revving of the engines as if she was sitting at my side and giggling into my ear. That was all it took for me to glance in whatever direction the sound had come from, and the moment I took my eyes off the course, I crashed. Each and every time. We ran six races before calling it a night.

"Ole non-driving ass boy!" Monie teased as we walked toward my car two hours after we'd arrived.

Our hands were linked, and the feel of her soft palm pressed against mine made it impossible for me to feel anything but contentment.

Grinning, I nodded. "G'on 'head and yuck it up."

Tossing her head back, she laughed. "Don't mind if I fucking do." Her eyes twinkled with mirth. "Ole make-a-left-at-the-ditch ass boy! Ole 'Hey, who put this wall here?' ass boy!" With her free hand, she clutched at her stomach, wheezing with laughter. I squeezed her hand.

"It's all good. Get these jokes off while you can because I'mma be spanking that ass on Saturday when we pull out the dominoes." The weeks had flown by, and the February kickback was a week away.

We approached my car, and I opened the passenger door, but instead of climbing inside, Monie turned to me, sucking her teeth.

"I'm supposed to believe that when you could have been spanking this ass earlier but opted out on some scary shit?"

"Wow," I drawled, biting back a laugh. "You really tryna play me right now, knowing damn well that if I woulda spanked that ass, we wouldn't have made it here—or anywhere else—tonight."

Stepping closer to me, she wrapped her hands around my waist and dropped her hands to my ass, gripping me with both palms.

"You say that like it's a bad thing."

"It is when I'm trying to date you."

She blinked a couple of times, making me chuckle before I leaned forward and pressed a quick kiss to her parted lips.

"Look at that shit. On hush-mouth."

That seemed to thaw her from her frozen state, and she rolled her eyes before climbing into the car. All I could do was laugh as I rounded the vehicle and climbed behind the wheel.

"You mad now?" I queried as I exited the raceway parking lot and took the ramp onto the highway.

Hands folded in her lap, Monie shook her head. "Not at all. I'm just thinking about all of the fucking I've done over the years with men I've called myself dating."

Amused, I shook my head. She was bothered, and a bothered Monie was a petty Monie. I relaxed in my seat, steering with one hand as I reached across the car and palmed the back of her neck, rubbing at the few tendrils of hair that had escaped the two buns she'd twisted her hair in.

"We've fucked, Mo."

Cutting her eyes at me, she sucked her teeth again. "We've *fucked*, Vick. One time. Singular."

"Nah, man. It may have been one night, but it was definitely more than once."

Rolling her head to face me, she gave me a rude look, making me laugh. She wasn't just mad; she was big mad.

"What happened between us leaving your spot and now? I thought we talked about this already."

Folding her arms across her chest, she shrugged and pressed her head into my hand.

"The horny never went away. Your little joke reminded me of how you held out."

I snorted, nodding as I exited the highway and eased to a stop at the red light on the feeder. "Duly noted."

From the corner of my eye, I saw her bite her lower lip as she eyed me. Just as I was about to ask her what was up, she slid a hand onto my thigh. For a moment, she just held it there unmoving, but then she began to slowly rub from my knee upward and then back down, brushing just below the spot where my dick was tucked against my thigh. Loosening the strap across her chest, she leaned over the console and slid a finger under my chin to turn my face to hers, giving me a firm kiss that was full of promise and intention. Pulling back, she stared into my eyes.

"In case it wasn't explicitly clear, I want this dick when we get back to my apartment."

Feeling light as hell, I grinned and dipped my chin once.

"Oh, I remember. Two dicks and one mouth, right?"

Grinning, she nodded as I winked at her.

"I got you, Mo. Let me get some dinner in you, and then I promise you can have all the dessert you want."

Her eyes flashed as she glanced at my lips again, but the timing was wrong. We were at a traffic light, and cars were behind me. The light turned green, but I waited until she settled in her seat before pulling into the intersection. I drove us to a town center on the west side. There were five restaurants to choose from, all scattered throughout the outdoor shopping mall that surrounded a large green space where a live band played jazz-rock. We walked hand-in-hand, fingers intertwined as we tried to decide which restaurant to choose.

After reading the menu posted on the outside of the third choice, we walked away and headed for the fourth restaurant when Monie suddenly stiffened at my side and snatched her hand from mine. Confused, I turned to her with furrowed brows.

"You okay?"

Her eyes were wide and trained on something over my shoulder. She took a couple of steps away from me, and when I aimed to follow, she quickly shook her head, making me halt my steps.

"Aye, Vick!" I heard yelled from behind me.

When I glanced over my shoulder and spotted Shad and Aisha headed our way up from across the street, I smiled and waved at them, but inside, my stomach plummeted. Their appearance was the cause for Monie's drastic change in behavior. I didn't want to believe it, but it was too much of a coincidence. After a couple of cars passed, our friends made their way over to us. I first hugged Aisha before slapping hands with Shad and pulling him in for a hug.

Once greetings were issued, they stood back, and I couldn't help but notice how they were holding hands while Monie and I were now standing at least two feet apart. Both my head and my heart hurt.

"What are *y'all* getting into?" Aisha asked slyly. It was a simple enough question, and could even be considered innocent, but there was something about the inflection in Aisha's tone that let me know neither of those had been her intention.

While I wanted to tell our friends that we were

just about to grab dinner to cap off our date, I knew from Monie's extreme reaction to seeing them that would be a bad idea. But before I could even give a watered-down version of the truth, Monie spoke up.

"We ran into each other at the go-kart place off I-45 and decided to get some dinner before we each went home, or to wherever Vick is going after."

Shad's eyebrows shot up and he shot me a questioning look, which let me know that I wasn't tripping. Monie's overly detailed lie was so damn obvious that it was almost worse than telling the truth. I couldn't even answer Shad's look with one of my own, because I'd turned to Monie, staring at the side of her face in complete disbelief. It was bad enough that she wanted to act like we weren't there together, but to infer that I was embarking on a night of who-knows-what instead of ending up in bed with her grated at me. It hit just like that comment she'd made after her event. The one where she implied that everyone in the crew had somebody, but I didn't count because all I did was "talk". It was a slug, pure and simple.

Aisha frowned. "You went to the go-kart place without me?! We've been talking about going there for weeks!"

"It was last minute," Monie lied, moving to pull Aisha into a hug, resting her chin on top of Aisha's head, something she did often and was easy enough with the eight-inch height difference between them. "I'm sorry, Eesh. Don't be mad at me."

Rolling her eyes, Aisha looked over at me. "Let me guess, you decided to go at the last minute too?"

I shook my head and shoved my hands into my pockets. "Nah, I was on a date."

Aisha gasped and Monie's eyes widened. Shad took in both of their expressions and then shot another glance my way, this one narrowed and calculating. He was smart enough to piece together clues to figure out what went unsaid. Without a doubt, I'd be hearing from him later.

"You went on a *date*, Vick? Oh my gosh!" Aisha exclaimed, full of excitement as she bounced on her toes. "You never go on dates. Who'd you go with? Did y'all have a good time?"

"We did," I answered, smoothly ignoring the identity inquiry. "At least I thought so, but she must have decided I wasn't shit because she disappeared on me right before I could take her to dinner."

"Damn, that's tough," Shad sympathized, clapping a hand on my shoulder.

Tough was an understatement. I shrugged. "It is it what it is.

We fell into silence for a few moments before Monie patted her stomach, changing the subject to the reason we were all there in the first place. Shad and Aisha were searching for a place to eat as well, so we all decided on the Italian place at the southern end of the town center, and grabbed a table of four.

Thankfully, Monie turned off her theatrical debut, returning to her regular self during dinner. It was a relief, but because my mood had soured on the sidewalk, I couldn't fully enjoy sharing the meal with friends. It wasn't rare to spend time with the couple outside of our regular Saturday kickbacks, but this was essentially a double-date, and as Aisha put it, dating was something I didn't often do, so it should have been a big deal.

After everyone was sufficiently stuffed, we exited the restaurant and stepped back onto the sidewalk. The sun had descended completely and the lanterns that dotted the cobbled street on either side were lit. There was a soft breeze blowing, a few people dancing to the music, and a handful of couples sitting on blankets on the grassy area. The whole scene was picturesque and a wonderful place to end a date.

"Where'd y'all park?" Shad asked as we moved a few steps away from the front of the restaurant.

I nodded toward the west side of the town center. "I'm over behind the department store."

Aisha turned to Monie. "Where'd you park?"

"Yeah," I intoned dryly, canting my head to see her face. "Where'd you park, Mo?"

Giving Aisha the fakest, brightest smile I'd ever seen, Monie pointed west. "I'm over by Vick."

Nodding, Aisha hugged Monie tightly before wrapping her arms around my waist and peering up at me.

"You're walking her to her car, right?"

I shoved her toward her boyfriend. "What the hell kinda question—"

Laughing loudly, Shad grabbed Aisha. "I can't even be mad that you got mushed for asking that crazy shit."

Eyes wide, Aisha held her hands palm-up in the air. "What?! How was that a crazy question?"

"Damn, Eesh. Do you honestly believe I'd let Mo alone walk to her car at ten o'clock at night when I'm *right here*?"

"Well, not usually," she admitted, "but Monie made it seem like you were getting into something after dinner and I just wanted to make sure you put your friends before pussy." She pinned me with what she thought was a knowing glance, but all she'd done was further twist the knife that Monie had already shoved in my back.

Fuming, I glowered at Monie, hoping that she understood the damage she was doing to my character in her apparent fear of being seen with me romantically.

Remorsefully, Monie shook her head and held up her hands. "That's my bad. He never said he was going anywhere after dinner. I don't know why I said that."

Aisha's frown became a scowl, and she reached forward to slap at Monie's arm.

"Heifer, how dare you!"

Giggling, Monie backed out of Aisha's range. "I said 'my bad'!"

"Whatever!" Shifting apologetic eyes toward me, Aisha pouted. "I'm sorry, Vick. I should have never doubted you."

Giving a nonchalant lift of my shoulders, I dipped my head in acknowledgment. "I get it, baby doll. Chicks before dicks."

A contemplative look came over Shad's face. "I thought it was bros before hoes."

"It was," Aisha agreed, "but…who'd be the hoe in this situation?"

"Obviously, I'm the damn hoe!" I yelled, throwing my hands into the air in exasperation. "At least, according to Mo."

Rolling her eyes, Monie laughingly declared, "I said 'my bad' dammit! How many times do I have to say it? My. Fucking. Bad!"

"Aight, man. We outta here." Shad held his fist out, nodding when I dapped him up. "I'mma get at you later." His brows were raised, letting me know exactly what he'd be getting at me about.

I smirked. "Not tonight though. I don't need to hear you hitting a falsetto while Eesh blows your back out."

Aisha screamed and Shad sputtered with laughter.

"Bro, what the actual fuck?! Dawg, you dumb as hell."

Covering her face, Aisha whined, "Vick! Why are you like this?"

Shad cradled her against his chest. "Baby, don't even ask. Let's just go."

With a final wave, they walked off, wrapped in each other's arms, leaving me and Monie to stand on the sidewalk watching them. A pang of longing hit me in the chest, and I wished I could be all hugged up like that, but then I remembered why I couldn't and anger consumed me once more.

"We should probably get out of here now before they get to their car and Aisha demands Shad drive around to make sure I truly walked you. I'm sure you don't want them to see you in my car."

"Vick..."

I waited for her to finish, but she trailed off.

Without looking her way, I started walking. She fell into step beside me and we made the journey back to my car in complete silence. It was such a stark difference from when we'd first arrived that it made my head hurt. Even the ride back to her house was a quiet one, making me switch on some music just to keep from going crazy. The fact that Monie hadn't even offered an explanation made it glaringly obvious that she didn't see how fucked up her actions were.

Once we got to her apartment, I walked her to the door and turned to leave. We hadn't said a word to each other in more than forty minutes and I didn't see a need to force a conversation that she couldn't see as necessary.

"Wait. You're not coming in?"

Monie's voice stopped me in my tracks. Brows furrowed, I slowly spun on my heel to face her. She stood in her open doorway, a look of confusion on her face.

"No. I'm not."

"But..." She shifted her weight from one foot to the other. "I thought we were gonna..." she trailed off again.

A wry chuckle escaped my lips as I shook my head. Of course. It was fine if we fucked on the low, but God forbid our best friends saw us out on a date.

The worst part was how my dick was already getting hard at just the thought of entering Monie's home and sliding between her thick thighs.

Was it worth it though, if my heart got crushed in the process?

Apparently, I was thinking about it too hard for too long, because Monie crossed back over the threshold of her apartment to walk toward me. She grabbed my hand and led me inside, and just like that, the decision was made.

SEVEN

KICK, PUSH, TUMBLE

"I was wondering when you were going to show up," Darwin chuckled as he stood back so that I could enter the foyer of his house.

Glancing at my watch, I frowned. "What are you talking about? The game doesn't start for another hour. I'm early as shit." I followed him through the living room and into his man cave.

"You're not that early. I figured you would've wanted at least two hours to discuss Monie."

He plopped down onto one of the reclining chairs and grinned as if he'd solved a fucking mystery. Shad's sentimental ass must've already told Darwin what he'd witnessed. It was the Sunday after mine and Mo's half-cooked date, and Shad and I had planned to meet up at Darwin's to watch some college ball.

Taking a seat, I shook my head. "I don't need that long."

"Hold that thought!" Shad entered the room at a jog, rubbing a paper towel over his damp hands. "I need to hear this."

Darwin laughed. "I thought you already knew everything."

"Hell nah! I know what I *saw*. I have no idea what's going on behind closed doors."

"And what exactly did you see?" I asked, pulling a lever at my side and reclining my seat. Leaning back, I folded my hands behind my head and gave him an expectant look.

"I saw you get your feelings hurt and prepare to do the same thing I did when I almost lost my woman."

"Damn!" Darwin quipped, grabbing the bottle of beer from the cup holder on his chair and taking a swig. "That's tough."

Shad nodded. "That's the same thing I said to him, of course, I didn't realize it was about Monie when I said it."

"First of all," I interjected, "the difference between us is that you finessed your way into the pussy and fell in love when you were in it. You almost lost your woman cause you ain't wanna use your words like a big boy."

Darwin shouted with laughter as Shad flipped me the bird.

"I, on the other hand, have been upfront with this woman from the jump. I told her straight up that I wanted to be her man. She's the one playing me the fuck out." My lip curled as I rehashed the memory from that night. "And *hell yeah*, my feelings were fucking hurt! We were supposed to be on a damn date, and yet she tried to make me seem like a gentleman of the night or some shit."

"Gentleman of the night?!" Shad screeched, sitting up in his chair as he began to wheeze with laughter. "Bro, you wildin'."

Sucking my teeth, I reclined in my seat and tossed my arm over my eyes. "You heard her, Shad! She basically called me a fucking escort."

Shad shook his head slowly, giving me an incredulous look. "Nah…I must've missed that part, bro."

My brother chuckled and took another swig of his beer, eyes filled with mirth as he eyed me over the brown glass bottle. "I been told your ass not to go there."

Lifting my arm, I glared at him. "I was fifteen, my nigga! That shit don't count!"

"Wait! Hold the muthafuckin' phone!" Shad leaped out of his seat and rushed to the front of the room, pointing a finger at me as he turned to Darwin.

"Are you telling me this thing between him and Mo isn't new?" He peered at me, utterly gobsmacked. "You mean to tell me that y'all niggas clowned *me*, but *you've* been after Monie for long enough to gain a ruby?!"

Quirking a brow, I stared at him in silence, waiting for him to explain that shit because I was confused. When Darwin burst out laughing, I squinted, scrutinizing them both. Somebody was going to come off of an explanation.

He held his palm out toward Shad. "You ain't playing, I see. Engaged twelve minutes and already researching anniversary stones. It's a good look, bro."

Grinning, Shad slapped Darwin's hand before shooting a glance in my direction.

"Every year of marriage has a gem," he offered after likely noticing that I wasn't comprehending his reference. "Rubies are for the fifteenth year of marriage."

"Ah," I murmured, realizing what Darwin had been implying. I nodded. "That's what's up."

Shad just stood there staring at me unblinkingly, and when I realized that he was still waiting on acknowledgment, I laughed.

"*Maaaan*," I drawled, "I didn't clown you."

Squinting, he lifted his chin. "You bet on me though."

Grinning, I shook my head. "I know it was a year ago, but try to keep up. If I had to pay Doo Doo Brown, it's because I lost. If I lost, that means I bet in your favor. C'mon, dawg. You're too damn smart to be so slow."

At the nickname, Darwin chucked a bottle cap at my head with one hand and flipped me a single bird with the other. "That's why Monie don't want your raggedy ass."

My laughter dried up quicker than dew in one hundred degree weather when he said that shit and my lip curled in disgust.

"Fuck you, bruh."

Having obviously struck a nerve, he howled. "Call your girl." His eyes ballooned. "Oh wait, you can't!"

He was laughing so damn hard that his face was flushed. Shad gave me a sympathetic look before patting me on the shoulder and reclaiming his seat.

"Sorry, bro," he offered in a sincere voice.

Nah," I countered with a shake of my head, "that's the one thing she *will* do."

A loud snort made me glare in my brother's direction. Both noticing and yet completely ignoring the mean mug, he waved.

"I told your ass."

"That was fifteen years ago!" He had to let that

shit go. We weren't kids anymore. He was no longer the junior in high school trying to warn me, a freshman, off of his classmate.

"Time is inconsequential," he uttered with a dip of his chin as if his ass was Yoda or some shit. "Evident by you sitting in my house, crying about a broken heart."

"I can't believe this shit," Shad muttered, dragging my heated glare from my brother over to him. He sat on my other side, shaking his head in disbelief.

"What can't you believe?" I asked, deciding not to respond to my brother.

"I can't believe y'all gave me shit when you've been over here like...*this* for so damn long." He gestured in my direction, waving his hand up and down to indicate my current state.

Darwin shrugged. "I told him don't do it."

Groaning, I dragged my hands down my face. "Shut the fuck up, Danger Mouse! So what if you said that shit back then? It's been damn near two decades and I still did the shit. Now fucking what? Say something else, my nigga!"

"Uh..." Shad looked back and forth between us and if I squinted and leaned forward a few millimeters, I could see the question form on his face word for word. "What exactly did you tell him, Darwin?"

"I told his ass not to mess with Mo. You know

how shit was when we were in school, man. She would chew dudes up and spit them out. Nobody was good enough to last longer than a week with her —and to be honest, even that was too long for some of those busters that tried getting at her back in the day. It only got worse in college when she started getting into makeup."

Shad nodded. "Oh, I remember that. Man, dudes would wild out. I remember having to knock a few heads in behind her." He glanced at me. "And Vick was always down to ride on a clown." Trailing off, his look became contemplative, as if seeing the history in a brand new light.

"Yeah, man," Darwin continued. "But even before then, Vick had stars in his eyes for her. I told him the same thing that I told you; no matter how good they look, our friends should stay friends. Unlike your ass, he listened. At least until now."

"And also unlike Shad's ass," I interjected, "I didn't come over here looking for advice from you, so we can dead this shit right here." He wasn't even offering advice, just looking to have his ego stroked by reminding me that he'd called this.

He stared at me for a moment before lifting his hands into the air in surrender. "I can see that you're broken up about this, so I'll leave it alone." I almost took a sigh of relief but knowing my brother like I did, he was incapable of leaving shit alone unless he said his peace. When he took a breath, narrowed my eyes.

"All I'll say," he added, "is that I never wanted to see you get hurt, which is why I warned you in the first place. If you keep running behind Mo like a puppy, you're guaranteed to get your tail stepped on. Monie thinks like a dude in a lot of ways. If she doesn't feel like it's her idea, she won't rock with it. I know how you feel about her, but you might need to back down. If y'all are meant to be together, then it'll happen."

After that, he unmuted the eighty-inch flat-screen on the wall and let the subject drop. Thankfully, Shad held onto his two cents, and I was able to watch a few games in pretend peace. Despite not going to him for advice, Darwin's words rang in my ears for a while. It was the song that wouldn't end, all the way up to and throughout the next kickback, which was the following Saturday.

The March kickback was at Monie's apartment, and I timed it so that I pulled up right as Shad and Aisha were getting out of Shad's car. After showing love to both of them, Shad gave me a questioning look, asking if I was good without uttering a word. I nodded, assuring him that I was fine.

The show that Monie worked on was

approaching their one-hundredth episode and because of that, Monie had another incredibly busy week. The time had allowed me to examine what we were doing and whether or not we should—or even could—move forward. I knew what I wanted the answer to be, but I felt like Monie was hard to read.

Except...she wasn't. If I paid attention to her actions instead of just focusing on what I wanted, it was as clear as freshly cleaned glass what Monie wanted. Because of that, I relaxed quite a bit. I was still my regular self, but more subdued when it came to her. I didn't even treat her the same as usual because traditionally, that managed to teeter the line of suggestive or inappropriate. I spent the entire kick-back reeling myself in when I came in contact with her, and it was as much for my benefit as it was for hers.

If being seen with me made her uncomfortable, I would be considerate by keeping my distance. It was a two-fold strategy for me, since appearing platonic in front of our friends meant that things wouldn't be awkward for anyone after I shut shit down between us.

When the day wound down, we all pitched in with the cleaning. Shad ran the vacuum while Aisha helped Lisette wrap up the last of the food. Darwin broke down the foldable tables that we'd used, and

Monie went to toss the tablecloths into the washing machine as I took out the trash. When I returned, everyone but Lisette was gone. I tried to walk out with her, but she hugged me and told me to stay until Monie came out of the laundry room.

"This feels like a setup," I noted.

Instead of reassuring me, she simply smiled and reached up to pat my cheek before leaving the apartment and closing the door behind her. The moment that the door snapped shut, Monie reappeared from the laundry room, which was through her small, galley kitchen.

"Is everybody gone?" She glanced around the room, and when she noticed it was just us, smiled and crossed the space to wrap her arms around my neck without waiting for an answer.

"I feel like I haven't seen you in forever," she murmured, pressing her lips to mine for a kiss.

Despite how that simple act knocked the second-to-last shred of hope out of me, I knew that if I put my hands on her the way I wanted to, I wouldn't be leaving her apartment any time soon. Mentally scolding myself, I rested my hands on her waist to keep from gripping her ass, and leaned back, breaking the kiss.

"Yeah, everyone's gone and we got your place righted, so I'm heading out too."

Eyes boring into mine, she gave me a searching look. "I haven't seen you in almost two weeks but we finally get a moment alone and you want to leave?" Her pitch fluctuated up and down as if she found the situation not only unbelievable but comical as well.

Annoyed, I reached up and removed her hands from around my neck. "Yeah. I need to get to the gym before it gets late and too crowded, so I gotta get going."

The look she gave me was full of incredulity.

"The gym," she said dryly. "You're passing on my pussy to go lift weights?"

Frowning, I held up a hand. "Let me stop you right there. I'm not passing up on shit. I'm choosing not to do this with you anymore because it's not what I want."

Her eyes widened, and she took a step back from me. "Wow. You chased me, and now you don't want me? Ain't that some shit?"

Frowning, I held up a hand. She was taking this way too far, entirely too damn fast. "Nah, Mo. Stick to the facts. I didn't chase you just to fuck, and you know that. I pursued you because I love you. I told you I wanted to be your man because it's all I've ever wanted to be. *Not* this shit I let you turn me into. I never wanted to be the man you fuck in private but pretend not to know in public, so I'm putting an end to it."

Seemingly stunned, she gaped at me.

"Don't worry," I offered amicably, somehow managing to hold my shit together even though I was broken as fuck and bleeding on the inside. "I won't blow up your spot just because this shit didn't work out the way I'd hoped. It'll be just like nothing ever happened." When she still didn't say a word, I blew out a breath through my nose.

She was rooted in place, so I crossed the two feet that separated us, slid my hand over the back of her neck, and dropped a kiss on her forehead. And because she was staring at me with those big, brown eyes—and I just couldn't help myself—I dropped a kiss onto her lips as well.

"I'll holla at you later."

EIGHT

WHY DON'T YOU BE MY GIRLFRIEND

I don't know what I'd been expecting, but Monie's response—no—her *lack* of response fucked me up. Actually, that's a lie. I know exactly what I was expecting from her. I was expecting her to say that she understood where I was coming from and that she felt the same way. That she not only loved me too, but had been waiting for me to say something and couldn't wait to spend the rest of her life with me. I'd hoped that Monie would tell me that the sex was just a bonus because she couldn't imagine us staying in some weird friends-with-benefits situationship since her emotions had changed.

I should've listened to Darwin's annoying ass because here I was now, with my feelings hurt yet again, looking like a damn fool. After being the funny man all of my life, finally, the joke was on me.

Instead of going straight home, I did like I'd told Monie, and went to the gym to work out some of the anger, and all of the hurt, that I felt. As I ran on the treadmill, I thought back on everything that'd transpired between us over the last few months. From the last kickback of the year to tonight, I couldn't even honestly say that I hadn't seen this coming. At nearly every point in my pursuit of Monie, she seemed hesitant to go all-in.

And try as I might to forget it, the episode at the town center drove home the point like Mario Andretti was behind the wheel. There was no way to deny that, despite how sweet and loving she was when we were alone, it didn't mean shit if she wasn't willing to replicate that behavior in public. Or hell, even in front of our friends. They were probably the only people on earth who would get how we fit together.

Shaking my head, I upped my speed and ran harder, pounding my feet against the machine as if I could outrun my failure. After more than an hour of running, I realized that it was impossible. The piece of equipment I was on was stationary, just like mine and Monie's relationship—if it could even be called that—and no matter what I did, there was no way to move it forward. It was a hard pill to swallow, but it was necessary all the same.

I told your ass.

Darwin's words echoed in my head once more, only serving to make me angry at myself. *How the fuck was I supposed to know that shit from the ninth grade would still be relevant?*

Defeated, I gradually slowed down my speed until I was walking at about five mph, waiting for my heart rate to slow down so that I could jump off the machine and make my way home.

I didn't even bother flipping on a light switch once I stepped inside of my empty apartment, not wanting even a shred of light to disturb the dark mood that I was in. Weaving through the maze of my furniture, I made my way through the open door of my bedroom. I shuffled into my bathroom, kicking the door closed behind me before stripping and jumping into the shower. After failing to wash my emotions down the drain, I stepped out of the bathroom with a towel wrapped around my waist and promptly started at the sight of Monie sitting on my bed, holding the jar of coconut oil that I usually kept in my bathroom cabinets.

"Wha–"

"I'm sorry."

Surprised, my eyebrows shot toward the ceiling. An apology was on the shortlist of things that I didn't believe Monie to be capable of—whether I believed her to be in the wrong or not. Hell, Shad had given up waiting on her to own up to how she'd dressed him down when things between him and Aisha were on shaky ground. No longer a possessor of hope, I was curious what made the proudest woman I know do something so out of character.

"Why would you–"

"Can I put this on you?" Monie said abruptly, lifting the jar into the air. "I promise to talk while I do it, but you really need to moisturize while your skin is still damp."

The Boss was always on the clock. Before I could stop it, a smile tugged at my lips. To hide it, I rubbed a hand over my chin and dropped my chin to my chest, staring at my feet while I shook my head. I'd be lying if I said I didn't want to hear what she had to say. My brain and heart were once again at war, and because of that, I found my feet carrying me over to the bed, where I stopped in front of her. Lifting my head, I attempted to meet her gaze, but her eyes were already on my body. Unscrewing the lid of the jar, Monie dipped her fingers into the softened oil and rubbed it between the palms of her hands until it liquefied. Then she stood to her feet and rounded my body, placing her hands on my shoulders.

"Just... Let me get this out before you say anything. Please."

When I didn't say anything, she took that as her key to continue.

"Thank you. I'm gonna say this again, just in case it didn't hit like it should have the first time. *I'm sorry*. I know that I hurt you earlier, but I promise you that it wasn't my intention. I know this is gonna sound like bullshit, but I just needed time to think."

Twisting my neck, I peered back at her with my face scrunched in confusion.

"What'd you need to think about?"

Poking me in the cheek, she turned my face back toward the bed. "Okay, hardhead. I definitely asked your ass to let me finish before you said something. You gonna do that or nah?"

Silently, I stared at the wall across the room, but this time a nonverbal response wasn't good enough for her. Sucking her teeth, she thumped me on the shoulder.

"Answer me," she demanded in a firm voice.

Though she couldn't see me, I pursed my lips and blew out a breath through my nose. "Man, go ahead."

"Thank you," she responded primly. Reaching around me, she dipped her fingers back into the jar, this time, rubbing the heated oil over the skin of my lower back, around my waist, and up my ribs.

"It seemed like things changed between us overnight, even though I know that's not how it happened. I felt like, one day, we were all chillin' at a kickback, and the next, you had me bent over the foot of my bed." She sighed, and suddenly, I felt her hands on my calves. "That was a hell of a transition, Vick, and while you didn't even blink, I needed to process that shit. Sometimes, it didn't even seem real."

I stood stock-still as she kneeled in front of me and massaged the oil into my legs and feet.

Gripping her elbows, I helped her onto her feet before dropping my hands to my sides as she started on my chest.

"I'm not used to you being serious about anyone. In all the years that I've known you, I personally never saw you move a woman from the talking stage to the relationship stage." Eyes on my chest, she shrugged one shoulder. "So, as much as I loved the attention from you, why would I think it would be different for me?"

I'd been able to stay silent up until then, but I couldn't let that one slide. My jaw was tight as I grunted, "That's not a real question."

Snapping her eyes up to my face, her lashes fluttered as she blinked a few times in confusion.

"How is that? I asked it, didn't I?"

"Nah, you made a false inference and tried to mask it as a question."

Jerking her neck back, she narrowed her eyes at me. "Excuse me?"

Ignoring the warning in her tone, I doubled down. "You don't have to wonder whether or not things would be different for you, because they already were. Even before I kissed you on New Year's, you knew it was something different. And even when you tried to pretend that things weren't changing between us, I was still there, showing you that they were. Don't try to use my dating history as an excuse when the reality is that you were scared."

I paused, expecting her to go off on me for that accusation, but when she gaped at me with wide eyes, I pressed on.

"Just like I never got serious with anyone, neither did you. That means something to me, Mo. It tells me that we both knew the people we were fucking with weren't our soulmates, and we'd rather stay single than settle for less. Every single one of those wack-ass dudes you've let take you on dates or smell your pussy in the past were less because I'm your more. You can't keep running from that."

"*Vick*," she uttered thickly, "I don't want to run from it. That's why I'm here. My actions earlier and on our date may not have shown it, but I love you, Vick. I swear that I do."

Her voice was thick with emotion, and my chest

tightened in response. I swallowed hard against the lump that was trying to form in my throat and turned my head, trying to focus on the curtains covering the window so that I wouldn't have to stare Monie in the face. There was a disconnect between my heart and my brain. My heart was ecstatic and wanted me to lift her into my arms and kiss her senseless.

Conversely, my brain was skeptical. It was one thing for her to declare love for me in the privacy of my bedroom, where no one could hear or see her, but it was a wholly different thing for her to put those words into action in front of the people whose opinions meant the most to her. The joy burgeoning inside of me was impossible to control, but I didn't have to let her see it.

Plan thwarted, she slid her warm, coconut-scented hands over my cheeks within seconds and redirected my attention, gently twisting my head until I was once again facing her. Our gazes clashed, and the glossy sheen over her brown eyes brought a pang to the center of my chest. The sincerity swimming in those depths was hard to ignore.

"This is hard as fuck for me, Vick. Talking to you has me emotional as hell," she swallowed audibly, frowning as if a mean mug would keep the gloss in her eyes from converting into tears, "and you know me… I'm a thug, and thugs don't cry, but here I am, about to become a blubbering fool just because I'm trying to tell you how much I love your silly ass."

Unbidden, a grin started at the corners of my mouth and grew rapidly. She'd said it twice now, and it wasn't so that she could convince me, but because it was her truth. And maybe, now that she'd uttered the words, they wanted to be heard again and again. Of all the things I wanted to do right then, complaining about that wasn't one of them.

"Your soft ass ain't no damn thug. You just want people to think that."

"I'm a Southside gangsta!" she insisted, trying to hold onto her scowl, but failing beautifully.

"You're a Sour Patch Kid wrapped inside of a purple jellybean," I murmured as I rested my hands on her waist and pulled her body flush against my own, "and that's just one of the many reasons why love you."

Wrapping her arms around my neck, Monie cradled the back of my head and stared into my eyes. "I love you so much, Vick. It's so bad—" she broke off, her voice tightening. She shook her head and ran her fingers over the back of my neck. "These feelings I have for you are so intense that it's scary. The love alone feels like something that's always been a part of me and that *terrifies* me, but I'm powerless in the face of it. I'm in so deep that, at this point, running away isn't even an option because all I want to do is wrap myself up in it and let it comfort me."

Heart swelling with a love so great that I was currently incapable of putting it into words, I squeezed her waist and kissed her softly, resting my forehead against hers.

"That was poetic as fuck, Mo. Let me find out you been moonlighting at the spoken word cafe down the street from Franklin."

Using her nails, she gripped a small sliver of skin on my neck and twisted, causing me to yelp and yank my head out of her grasp.

"Fuck you," she muttered, the wide grin on her face contradicting her dark tone.

Smirking, I nodded. "Mmhm. That's all you want my ass for anyway."

She gasped, placing a hand to her chest as she leaned away from me.

"That isn't true! The first and second reasons? Ya damn skippy! But that's certainly not *all* of the reasons."

Tossing my head back, I howled with laughter.

"Damn, Mo. Tell me how you really feel."

Her lips curved into a sensual grin that had my laughter tapering off with a quickness.

"Oh," she murmured coquettishly, "do you want me to be honest?"

As I licked my lips and nodded, I could feel the blood rushing to my dick, which was concealed only by the towel around my waist.

"Honesty is the best policy," I responded, my heart pounding with anticipation.

Eyes on mine, she slowly sank into a squat, her hands gripping the cinched knot of the towel at my waist.

"Well...if I'm being honest, this thing won't feel official unless we seal it with a kiss."

I blinked and my towel was on the floor. My dick was in Monie's warm hands, and her plush lips were puckered, placing the softest of kisses to my tip before she loosened her jaw and swallowed me down.

"Ah, shit, Mo." The groan was out of my mouth before I could even process it.

"Mmhm," she hummed.

Grabbing my ass with both hands, she bobbed in front of me as if her boss was Death and she was one soul shy of her quota for the night. It felt like mere moments passed before I was groaning her name, my fingers tangled in her hair as I buried my dick as far in her mouth as it would go and came so hard that my vision blurred. I felt wrung out; my knees were weak, body heavy. Releasing me, Monie stood on her feet and grabbed me by the shoulders to turn me toward the bed.

"Lay down, baby," she rasped, her voice raw. "I'll be right back."

Before she could move away from the bed, I grabbed her by the back of her neck and pulled her face to mine. The kiss was chaotic, a clack of teeth and mash of lips and tongue, but I had no words for how I felt and could only show her physically. It was only the desperate need to drag air into my lungs that made me wrench my mouth from hers.

"Get on the bed, Mo."

Trying to back away, she shook her head. "Let me brush my teeth first. My face is a mess."

"I don't give a fuck about that shit. You look as beautiful as always. Now get your ass on this bed."

There was a bit of defiance in her eyes as she licked her lips, her hungry leer bouncing between my eyes and mouth. "And if I don't?"

"You're talking like I won't bend you right the fuck over..." I trailed off at the tendril of excitement that flared in her eyes at my threat.

She didn't answer me, nor did she move. That was an answer in and of itself. A wicked grin stole across my face, and I slid off of the bed on the side by my nightstand. Reaching into the top drawer, I pulled out a condom and sheathed my dick. Her eyes were on me the entire time that I made my way over to her, and I watched her chest heave as her breaths quickened with anticipation. When I stood in front of her, I settled my hands over her hips and trailed them up her body until I cradled her face in my hands.

"What do you want from me, Mo?"

A stuttered sigh escaped her lips and she reached up to grasp my wrists. "I want you to fuck me like your life depends on it."

That could absolutely be arranged.

"And then what?" I queried, knowing—hoping—there was more.

Her bottom lip trembled. Reflexively, I leaned forward and sucked it into my mouth, nibbling on it until she moaned and my dick twitched.

"And then," she breathed when I released her, her eyes closed as she leaned into my hands, "I want you to hold me in your arms and stare into my eyes as you make love to me until we're too exhausted to do anything but pass out. And when we wake up, I want you buried inside of me."

"And after that," I whispered, hoping to hear words that would not only arouse my body but comfort my heart.

Her eyes popped open, and she peered at me.

"After that, I want you to love me. And never let me go. And allow me to love you in return. I want to be yours, and I never want you to have to wonder if I want you to be mine."

When I didn't say anything after too many seconds had passed, Monie grabbed my wrists and squeezed.

"Did that answer your question?"

"Ye—" I cleared my throat, which was clogged with all of the feelings that the woman in front of me evoked, and tried again. "Yeah, Mo. That more than answered my question."

"Good." Her smile turned sultry as she nibbled on her bottom lip. "Now, about that first request…"

Smirking, I dropped my hands to her hips and began gathering the material of her dress in my hands.

"You ain't said nothing but a word."

ONE LAST THING

The April kickback came around faster than I liked. I mean, I loved spending time with my people, but I hated how the weeks seemed to fly by once Monie and I became an official couple. Although it was Lisette's turn to host, we were back at Darwin's crib because Lis had temporarily moved back in with her parents to cut expenses while she had a house built.

At Monie's request, I'd baked a caramel cake, which was her favorite. When we pulled up to my brother's house, she'd insisted on entering the house ahead of me as I pulled the cake from the floor in the backseat.

"I just want to make sure no one is in your way," she said with wide eyes that kept darting to the white box. "If someone bumps into you and ruins that cake, I'mma open up a can of whoopass."

"Aight, Mo," I'd conceded, chuckling at her dramatics. "Do what you gotta do, man."

Settling the cake on the roof of the car, I locked the doors and slid my keys into my front pocket. When I had the cake in my hand, I looked around to see that Monie was already halfway to the front door. By the time I'd made it onto the sidewalk, she'd already rang the doorbell, and when I started up the path that would lead me right to the porch, I saw my brother open the front door and pull her into a hug.

Though the timbre of his voice carried over to me, I couldn't hear what he said.

"Leave the door open!" Monie shouted as she passed by Darwin. "My man is coming in with my cake, and none of you muthafuckas better not so much as breath on it, or that's your ass!"

My steps faltered as I made it to the cement slab that was Darwin's porch, and my eyes collided with my brother's as we both registered Monie's unorthodox announcement at the same time. His brows flew toward his hairline, and the shock on his face brought a massive grin to my own.

"Aww shit!" Darwin exclaimed, extending his hand and pulling it back before swinging it toward me.

Shifting the cake to my left hand, I met his slap and accepted the handshake that immediately followed. Still gripping my hand, he pulled me into the house.

"How long has that been going on?" He nodded at Monie's retreating form.

"Officially or unofficially?"

He smirked. "Officially, smartass."

"About a month."

His eyes widened as realization set in, but then he just chuckled and shook his head.

"I see your ass still didn't listen to anything I told you, but it looks like it worked out, so congratulations."

"Nah, bro. I did listen. I backed off of her; called myself shutting the shit down."

He eyed me. "Mo just walked in here, telling the whole block that you're her man, so something had to change."

"Yeah, she changed. Or something changed for her, or whatever the fuck. I don't know. All I know is that I tried to dead the shit, but a couple of hours later, I step out of the shower and she's in my house."

"And now you're her man."

Grinning, I nodded. "If we're being real, I *been* her man, she just decided to finally tell y'all."

"Well, yeah, that's probably because it's *'official'* now."

He had a point, and I made sure to tell him so just before we stepped into the great room where the rest of our friends were already gathered. While Darwin headed for the cluster of seating, I shot Monie a wink and dipped off into the kitchen. Carrie was standing at the stove, stirring something in a pot that smelled amazing, so after sliding the cake onto the counter, I pulled her into a hug. She'd been attending more of our monthly get-togethers since Shad and Aisha hooked up, but hadn't been to the last few, so it was good to see her.

The food was already finished before we'd arrived, so everyone grabbed plates of spaghetti and sat around the living room as Darwin pulled out the playing card version of Battle Of The Sexes. The living room became loud and boisterous by the time we neared the end of the game. I fought tooth and nail, but the girls won. We were outnumbered, but they claimed it didn't help them, which was an obvious lie.

"Aww," Monie cooed as she returned to the couch and pressed herself against my side, pushing her titties against my bicep as she leaned down to nuzzle my neck, "what'sa matter with da baaaabyyy?"

Hearing her parrot the words I'd said to her the

night we first made love brought an immediate grin onto my face, which I tried to tamp down by canting my head away from her.

"Man, get outta here with all of that."

Giggling, Monie gripped my chin in her hand and turned my face toward her before dropping a firm but chaste kiss on my lips. "You gon take this ass whooping like a man, and tell me how proud you are of me for winning."

I stared at her, less annoyed as the seconds flew by as I absorbed the very public display of affection that she was putting on in front of our friends.

"Gimme another kiss." It was a command, but also a request.

Those brown irises seemed to melt as her eyes softened, making my chest tighten with need. Slowly, she extended her neck until our lips were scant millimeters apart.

"Say please," she whispered.

"Please."

The plea was barely audible over the groan low in my throat but she must've heard it well enough because she kissed me again. Feeling benevolent, it was slower this time, slipping her tongue into my mouth for the briefest of seconds before pulling back and grinning at me. Swiping my tongue over my lips, I smiled.

"I'm proud of you for cheating your way into a win. If that's what it takes for you to feel good about yourself, then I will support you because I love you and want you to be happy."

Her mouth fell open as her face contorted into shock, but then she blinked, yelped something like a battle cry, and shoved me away from her.

"You sore loser! You are such a big ass baby!" she exclaimed.

Laughing, I shook my head and scooted next to her, propping my chin on her shoulder. "Why I gotta be a baby just 'cause you cheating? How that work, Mo?"

"I'm just calling it like I see it. Pouting because your team lost fair and square is peak baby behavior, Vick."

"You love me, though," I quipped, knowing it didn't have a damn thing to do with the conversation but wanting to hear her say it.

Her lips curved up even as she gave me a side-eye. "I do."

"Look at my friends!" Lisette squealed, hugging herself. "Everyone is all loved up. It's so beautiful."

"Definitely is," Darwin chimed in as he collected the cards. "It's a good look for my people. Now we just need to find somebody that Lis wants to settle down with, and then the crew will be complete."

Smiling, Lisette shook her head. "Settling down is a *y'all* thing, not a *me* thing, so how about we don't and just say that we did?"

Raising his head, Darwin abandoned the cards he was putting into order and shot Lisette a look that I couldn't figure out.

"Are y'all ever gonna tell 'em?"

We all looked toward the kitchen where Carrie was fixing herself a second serving of spaghetti. It was almost like she hadn't spoken, the way she wasn't paying us any attention, using the tongs to fill her plate with pasta. Confused, I shot a glance around the room, trying to figure out who she was talking to. From the look on Monie's face, she had no clue either. The only people who didn't look lost were Lisette and my brother.

What the fuck?

Breaking the stare-down that she and Darwin were engaged in, Lisette burst out laughing and folded her arms over her chest, staring pointedly across the room at Carrie.

"Now, Carrie," she scolded in an airy voice, "why are you trying to start mess?"

"Yeah, man," I added cautiously, still unclear of Carrie's meaning. "Don't even play around with something like that. Behind Mama and Daddy, you and Deuce Bigalow are my model couple. Don't ruin that for a joke."

Walking back into the living room, Carrie gave me a cryptic smile. "Who's joking?"

Turning to my brother, I waited for him to confirm that his wife was just gone off the loose juice that Shad made, but all he did was smirk. My mouth fell open and I sat up straight. I knew damn well that Carrie wasn't saying what the fuck it sounded like she was saying, all for him to not even refute that shit.

"*Nigga,*" I whispered in a choked voice. I had no other words. The mere idea of what they were implying had me speechless.

"Damn, Lis," Monie breathed, sounding impressed, "who *haven't* you slept with?"

The odd way that she'd phrased that question made me swing my head toward her. Lisette was a free spirit, but that didn't mean she should be called a hoe, which is how Monie's question sounded. In lieu of a verbal response, Lisette lifted both of her index fingers and pointed one toward me and the other toward Shad. Immediately, he and I looked at each other. Without a doubt, the stupefaction I read on his face was surely mirrored on my own. I shot to my feet as if the couch was on fire.

"Now wait just a goddamned minute!" I yelled. "I

know damn well there weren't catfights going down without a referee!" Reaching into my back pocket, I retrieved my wallet and flicked open the flaps to pull out a tiny plastic baggie, which I lifted into the air.

"Exhibit A!" I announced, circling the coffee table. "One authentic Waffle House napkin containing signatures from six of the seven present parties." Slapping the baggie down onto the table, I searched each and every face in that living room. "Does no one have an answer for this?"

"Exactly!" Shad cosigned, glaring at Aisha, who was splayed out on the couch as she laughed her ass off. "You said you were just kidding about that!"

"I wa—was!" Aisha stuttered, laughter stealing her breath and bringing tears to her eyes. "A—bout… th—that time."

Gasping, Shad clutched his chest above his heart. "Lying by omission? That's what's we're doing now, baby?"

Carrie shook her head, giggling as she swirled pasta around her fork as if she hadn't incited chaos. "I know for a fact that at least one of those instances was refereed."

"Yo, what?!" I swung around, facing my brother, brows furrowed in accusation. "Is there something you need to share with the court?"

Darwin shook his head. "That's none of your business, bro."

With narrowed eyes, I glared at him. He still said nothing, so I rounded the coffee table and stood before Lisette, pinning her with an expectant look. Her lips were curved into a mischievous grin as she mimed zipping her lips closed and tossing a key toward Carrie, who pretended to catch it before tilting her head back and dropping the invisible key down her throat. After letting off a real—and audible—belch, she winked at Lisette and glanced around the room.

"My bad, y'all. I didn't mean to cause such uproar." She didn't sound apologetic in the least. Both the smile on her face and her tone of voice said she was incredibly amused by our reactions.

Waving at her, I said, "Don't apologize. You're not the one keeping secrets in the circle of trust."

A ring of laughter engulfed the room as I glared at my brother from under narrowed eyelids. From the little smirk he wore, it was obvious he wasn't going to answer any questions, but that'd never stopped me before. Opening my mouth, I prepared to lob another question around the room, but before I could say another word, a hand encircled my wrist, and Monie pulled me back down to the couch. Linking our fingers, she leaned into me.

"You're worried about the wrong thing," she laughed, her warm breath ghosting over my neck and causing the fine hairs to stand at attention.

Mind already on her, I slid an arm over the back of the couch behind her head and face her. "What should I be worried about then?"

Smiling, she brought her hand to the back of my head and rubbed her fingers over my scalp.

"Not a damn thing."

It wasn't what I expected her to say, but it was what I'd needed to hear. Sooner or later, I'd get the full story out of my brother, but at that moment, it didn't matter. What *did* matter was the woman sitting next to me, the people—my family—surrounding us, and the sheer contentment that I felt.

"You know what? You're absolutely right."

ABOUT THE AUTHOR

Chencia C. Higgins is just a girl from Texas writing about sassy, southern women finding love. With a multitude of titles under her belt, she has made it her mission to create stories in which Black women are loved out loud. In 2019 she won a Romance Slam Jam Emma award for her debut paranormal romance, Janine: His True Alpha. When she isn't hunkered down in her writing cave, Chencia can be found with her nose in a book (or two, or three), saving recipes on Pinterest, and traveling as much as possible with her family.

To be informed about future releases, events, and happenings, visit her website and join her mailing list.

www.therealchencia.com

http://eepurl.com/dhCDsz

 twitter.com/twitter.com

 instagram.com/ohchencia

 bookbub.com/authors/chencia-c-higgins